Sugar Coated
Lies

Jan Fields

Annie's®
AnniesFiction.com

Library of Congress-in-Publication Data
Sugar Coated Lies / by Jan Fields
p. cm.
I. Title
                    2016952052

AnniesFiction.com
(800) 282-6643
Chocolate Shoppe Mysteries˜
Series Creator: Shari Lohner
Series Editors: Janice Tate, Ken Tate
Cover Illustrator: Bonnie Leick

10 11 12 13 14 | Printed in China | 9 8 7 6 5 4 3 2 1

"Running over to Print Worthy," Jillian Green sang out as she wove her way among the worktables in the kitchen of The Chocolate Shoppe Bakery and snatched her jacket from the hook near the door. "I'll be back shortly." If anyone called out an objection, Jillian was moving too fast for the words to stick, and she made it out the back door before anyone managed to snag her.

After a long morning of mixed-success baking and decorating cupcakes for a preschool winter wonderland party, Jillian deserved a moment to herself to relish the chill of late January in Georgia. The cooler weather outside made the heat in the kitchen far more bearable, but that didn't mean she couldn't enjoy the initial cool, refreshing breeze tossing her long, auburn curls before pulling on a pale-blue knit hat to keep the breeze from tangling knots in her hair.

Thoughts of her morning spent making cupcakes brought a smile to her lips. She tried to keep a good attitude about her deathly slow improvements as a baker. After all, she hadn't set a fire in the bakery in months, and she was getting quite good at decorating, this time making dozens of miniature, iced polar bears. Looking at their tiny sugar faces gazing back at her had given her a flush of success, and she intended to hold on to that. It didn't happen very often.

She was flexing sore fingers from squeezing the icing bag and shaking them to release some tension when the quick honk of a car horn drew Jillian's attention sharply to the street beside her. A blue Volvo sailed past. Inside, Annalise Reed waved brightly, and Jillian raised her hand in reply, though she doubted Annalise saw it before she'd passed. Like several members of the Southern Sweetie Pies baking club, Annalise was a new friend but already a good one.

Shoving her hands into her jacket pockets, Jillian took a deep breath, then blew it out slowly and smiled in almost total contentment. She tried to take a walk every day while the cooler weather lasted, but it was hard with all the demands on her time. At least the crazy Christmas rush at the bakery had slowed down with the new year. The workload was finally something she, Lenora, and her grandmother, Bertie, could handle without whimpering. More than once, Jillian was ridiculously grateful that Lenora Ryan had stayed on with the bakery after Jillian came home. Jillian and Bertie could never have handled all the baking alone.

Moving home to Georgia from Los Angeles was supposed to let her escape from the high-pressure stress of the city, but despite the laid-back Southern attitudes around her, Jillian had found plenty of stress right there in the town of Moss Hollow, though it all seemed to be smoothing out.

Coming home had reminded her of all the things to love about the little town. As she continued down the sidewalk, meeting other people enjoying the pleasant weather, they nearly always looked her right in the eye and smiled. She got more eye contact in a short walk down the street than in a year of living in Los Angeles.

She glanced in the front window of Pearls Before Wine, a little vintage jewelry and accessories shop and noticed they still had cheerful Santas in the window display, despite the holiday being weeks past. In the South, the passage of time was more of a suggestion than a universal constant. In fact, when driving in to the bakery that very morning, she'd seen one house boldly lit with Christmas lights.

After her stroll up and down the street, Jillian stopped to pick up some brochures from the print shop across from the bakery.

When she stepped through the door of Print Worthy, she quickly unzipped her light jacket. For some reason, the shops in Moss Hollow seemed terrified of the cool, breezy winter weather and turned the heat to broil. It was almost cooler in the kitchen of the bakery than in the little print shop.

The owner looked up from her paperwork, and recognition spread over her face, her bright eyes nearly vanishing in an apple-cheeked grin. Jillian eyed Lisa Flint's short, dark hair with something akin to envy, thinking how much less effort it must be to tame close-cropped hair than the curly mane she had. The sleek, upscale California salon style she'd worn back to Moss Hollow was a thing of the past, and her hair had grown out to something better resembling a lion's mane.

Every spare cent Jillian had brought from California was going into sprucing up Belle Haven, the antebellum home she shared with her grandmother, Bertie Harper, and Bertie's twin sister, Cornelia Montgomery. They'd thrown themselves into it after Aunt Cornelia announced that she'd had a dream about returning the old mansion to its former glory. Although Aunt Cornelia was constantly having dreams or portents or plain old wacky ideas, Jillian had thought this particular dream sounded like a good idea. It would give them a chance to expand the catering side of the bakery business with some event planning, which played to Jillian's strengths as a former employee of an advertising agency better than her baking skills.

Unfortunately, remodeling and repairs ate money at an alarming rate. When Jillian had to cut back on things like visits to the hair salon, the penny-pinching became painful. She wondered if she should swing by the Clip & Curl for some emergency hair repair before the frizz took on a life of its own.

"I've finished your brochures." Lisa plunked a cardboard box on the counter, snapping Jillian out of her hair funk. "I was able to incorporate all the changes your grandmother asked for, but it was close. If she'd called any later, I would have had to do the whole print run again. Next time, please, finalize the copy a little sooner."

Jillian froze in the middle of reaching for the box. "Changes?"

Jillian had worked on the event brochure for over a week, poring over the text every night after dinner. She wanted to make the work on Belle Haven sound as good as possible without stretching the truth *too* much. The reality was that the women from her grandmother's baking club, the Southern Sweetie Pies, had gone above and beyond the call in helping Jillian get the house in shape for events. She never would have been able to do half as much if she'd had to hire it all out.

The club had scrubbed, peeled wallpaper, painted, and polished their way into heaven as far as Jillian was concerned. When they were done, there was a definite swath of elegance right down the middle of Belle Haven where visitors might be dazzled by all that the mansion once was. As long as no one wandered off that middle stretch, the house looked pretty good.

The Sweetie Pies weren't the only restoration angels in Moss Hollow. Aunt Cornelia's garden club had descended on the back garden and had done wonders that almost made Jillian believe in magic. But, as with the house itself, things definitely went downhill if guests ventured off the "beaten path." In the wilder areas of the back gardens, wanderers could end up in the swamp if they weren't right careful.

Staring nervously at the cardboard box on the counter, Jillian wondered why Bertie felt the brochures needed changes.

Lisa's smile weakened, and she quickly pulled a brochure from the box and held it out. "You didn't know about the changes Bertie requested, did you?"

Jillian forced cheer into her voice. "I expect she simply didn't think to tell me. I'm sure it's fine." She took the brochure and sighed softly in relief. At first glance, it looked exactly the way Jillian had envisioned. Bertie hadn't changed the layout or swapped out any of the soft-focused photographs of the house and gardens. The brochures looked as lovely as Jillian imagined.

Then she felt a sinking dread as she read the text: *After extensive remodeling, Belle Haven has returned to its original antebellum splendor.*

She certainly had *not* written that and doubted the house's "original antebellum splendor" involved keeping most of the rooms closed to prying eyes so that no one could see the limits of their remodeling budget. One look at the old two-story library would give a person nightmares involving killer dust bunnies and possibly bookworms—not the cute cartoon kind, either.

And the main parts of the house that Jillian intended to use for events did look lovely, but "original antebellum splendor"? She shook her head slowly in dismay. Sure, the updates to Belle Haven were nothing short of amazing considering most of the work was done by a group of women who were more at home with gingerbread houses than real ones, but her grandmother had definitely gilded the lily.

And the more Jillian read, the more gilding she spotted.

Let us host your upscale events, whether on a grand scale, or small and intimate.

Jillian swallowed the lump in her throat. *Where would we put everyone in a grand-scale event?* She hoped Bertie's exaggeration didn't come back to bite them later.

After she paid Lisa, Jillian hauled the surprisingly heavy box of brochures outside. Waiting for the traffic to clear so she could cross the street, she tried to work out whether it was worth arguing with Bertie about the changes. They were already in print, and she certainly couldn't afford to have them reprinted. Besides,

Jillian had spent years in advertising; she knew the changes her grandmother made were hardly the biggest exaggeration she'd ever seen. Gilding the lily was mild compared to some of the ad campaigns she'd seen, and had worked on, in California. By the time she reached the front door of the bakery, she'd talked herself down from all-out panic and decided to forget the whole thing and hope for the best.

With her hands full, she reached out with her elbow and managed to hook the door handle, pulling it open far enough to shove the toe of her boot into the crack. Then she used her leg to leverage the door open and squeezed in. She spotted Bertie standing in the middle of the dining area and frowned. Her tiny grandmother was smiling brightly at her, something Bertie rarely did.

"That's okay, Bertie," Jillian told her. "I can handle the box and the door." Bertie had always insisted that Jillian call her by her first name.

"I knew you could. You're a competent woman," Bertie said, watching Jillian as she crossed the room and dumped the box on one of the display counters. Jillian's grandmother looked even smaller than usual next to the tall, well-dressed woman beside her. "Come over here and meet Mrs. Blackwater, the mayor's wife. She has a job for us."

Jillian checked her hands quickly for ink or dust, and tried not to notice the state of her manicure. She shook the tall, stout woman's hand. Mrs. Blackwater wore an impeccably tailored cadet-blue suit with a frilly white blouse. A pillbox hat on her dark hair completed the Jackie Kennedy look that Jillian suspected the woman was after. "I'm pleased to meet you."

The taller woman nodded. "Your grandmother tells me upscale events were your specialty when you lived in California."

"I did assist in planning some large events in Los Angeles,"

Jillian said, "for the advertising agency where I worked."

"It was Jillian's experience that really inspired the whole idea," Bertie said, giving her granddaughter a fierce look for not going along with whatever play Bertie was making.

Jillian nodded hesitantly. It *was* her idea, sort of. And she thought it best not to mention her flaky great-aunt's dream message from her dead husband that put the stamp of approval on the plan, as least as far as Aunt Cornelia was concerned.

Jillian noticed Bertie was still giving her the patented grandmother death stare and decided to toss the ball back to her. "My grandmother is being modest and generous. My experience is minor compared to hers. The Chocolate Shoppe Bakery has catered events around this area for years."

"Of course." Mrs. Blackwater's smile was tight, pinching her carefully applied burgundy lipstick into a thin slash on her face. "Though I'm hardly talking about providing cupcakes for a child's birthday party."

Jillian snuck a glance at her grandmother and noticed the death glare had been turned on Mrs. Blackwater. Luckily, the mayor's wife didn't seem to notice as she continued to explain. "I want an *event*. I want you to plan my daughter's wedding. To be honest, I was hesitant to consider you, but we don't have a lot of time and my options were somewhat limited. The mayor, my husband, considers it important that the wedding be handled by local businesses and believes that you are capable of giving us the elegant affair we desire. He wants our daughter to be happy, of course, but he also recognizes the importance of appearances for a man in his position."

Jillian swallowed. It sounded like a big deal for their first event. "We usually work alongside the wedding planner," she said weakly. At least, the bakery had always worked with wedding planners when her grandmother had catered weddings in the past.

"Dreams Come True is an excellent wedding planner," Bertie chimed in. "I can recommend them wholeheartedly. We've worked with them before."

Mrs. Blackwater waved away the protest. "The wedding is an event, and your grandmother assures me that you're an event planner. That should certainly be something you can handle. I have no intention of throwing away money for another planner. My husband insists the wedding be elegant, impressive, and *cheap*. Cheap and local rather limited my options, which is why I'm willing to consider a business that is so newly expanded. I'm hoping you can bring an upscale experience at a reasonable price."

Jillian flashed a look at Bertie, suddenly feeling quite in over her head. She was saved from having to come up with an appropriate reply when the bakery's door flung open and a young woman with multicolored hair flounced in. Though thinner than Mrs. Blackwater, the newcomer had the same bone structure and long legs as the mayor's wife. "Mama! I can't believe you started discussions about my wedding without me! You knew I was going to be a little late."

Mrs. Blackwater turned to look at her and winced. "I thought you were going to the Clip & Curl to get your hair turned a nice, normal color again."

The young woman crossed her arms over her substantial bosom. "No. That's what *you* wanted. I love my hair and so does Gordon." She shot a look toward Jillian. "Are you the wedding planner?"

"I'm the event planner," Jillian said weakly.

"Fantastic," the young woman said. "I'm Alice Blackwater, soon to be Alice Liddell, and I want to have an *Alice in Wonderland*–themed wedding. I'll dress as Alice, and Gordon will be the Mad Hatter." She cut a glance toward her mother. "Mama can be the Red Queen. She's been practicing for the role all my life. And my darling kitty can play the Cheshire Cat! It will be wonderful."

"That sounds ridiculous. We are certainly not going to turn your wedding into a circus!" Mrs. Blackwater said sharply.

"But it's my wedding," Alice said, drawing the words out from a drawl to a whine and adding a stamp of her foot at the end.

"For which your father and I are paying."

Alice narrowed her eyes at her mother. "Daddy will let me. *He* wants me to be happy."

Mrs. Blackwater glared back her daughter with an identical expression. "Your father is the mayor of Moss Hollow. He does not want his daughter to have a wedding that makes us all look like fools. He expects you to remember who you are, Alice!"

"I'm sure we can come up with something that makes everyone happy," Bertie said, stepping between Mrs. Blackwater and her daughter. "All we need is a little time to brainstorm ideas, now that we have a sense of your needs."

Mrs. Blackwater's mouth snapped shut, and she looked at Bertie for a moment, then nodded. "I will expect the ideas to be tasteful and elegant, something befitting the daughter of Moss Hollow's mayor."

"Of course," Bertie said.

"The wedding is in late March, so I recommend you come up with these amazing ideas quickly," Mrs. Blackwater said, handing Bertie a piece of paper. "Here is some information you'll need about our preferred vendors and the guest list. We may make some changes to the guest list, but this should help get you started."

"Of course." Bertie took the papers without looking at them, and the tall woman swept out of the bakery, reminding Jillian of the Red Queen her daughter accused her of being.

Alice Blackwater looked from Bertie to Jillian with her eyes narrowed. "I want an *Alice in Wonderland* wedding, and I expect you both to back me up. My daddy will want me to be happy. Remember that."

Before Bertie could respond, the young woman spun and stormed out of the bakery in a perfect imitation of her mother.

"Well, they are an interesting pair," Bertie said, her gaze on the paper. "Like seeing two versions of the same person."

"We're doomed," Jillian whispered as she stared at the closed bakery door. "We are totally doomed."

For nearly two months, Jillian felt as if she were taking a crash course in tightrope walking. Anything Mrs. Blackwater chose, Alice was certain to despise—and Alice's choices sometimes drifted toward the bizarre. Trying to find the middle ground of contentment for both sent Jillian home with a headache most nights. Plus, the *Alice in Wonderland* theme led to some disquieting dreams where Mrs. Blackwater demanded frequently that Jillian's head be cut off for poor flower choices or guest list mistakes.

Finally, she found herself tumbled into the week of the wedding, for better or worse. Though Jillian still had a million details to finalize, she could almost see light at the end of the tunnel. She only hoped it wasn't attached to a train waiting to mow her over. At least the weather had been uncharacteristically mild and dry all week, lessening any panic about the gardens turning into swamps before the ceremony.

After a lengthy call with the florist to discuss painted roses in Alice's bouquet, Jillian walked into the living room of Belle Haven, clutching a binder full of wedding details to her chest, and collapsed on the cornflower-blue sofa next to her great-aunt. The lovely linen-covered sofa had been one of their best consignment shop discoveries. As with many of the pieces Jillian had picked out during the remodel, it straddled the line between a sleek, modern look and traditional cozy comfort. Two love seats in the room picked up the cornflower color among the flecks of color in their pale, tweedy upholstery.

Since they'd purchased the new furniture, Jillian had noticed how well the cornflower-blue sofa went with Aunt Cornelia's multitude of floral dresses. Today, her great-aunt wore a pale-pink dress with accents that matched the sofa almost perfectly. So perfectly, in fact, that Jillian was beginning to wonder if her aunt was coordinating her clothing choices to look good while sitting on the sofa. Though far from vain, Aunt Cornelia was much more appearance conscious than her endlessly practical twin sister. Not that Bertie dressed shabbily. She simply made sure to pick things that were attractive and practical for a woman who spent most days up to her elbows in flour.

The gardening hat perched on Cornelia's blonde curls—at age seventy-nine, both Bertie and Cornelia dyed their gray hair—suggested she had been working outside, getting the back garden ready for the rehearsal dinner, only a day away now. Jillian had hired Lenora's cousin, Virgil, to do much of the heavy lifting for her aunt, and they'd worked amazingly well together. Along with the occasional drop in from Cornelia's gardening club, they'd created an outdoor dining area that was sure to meet even Mrs. Blackwater's exacting standards.

Jillian frowned at the light coating of fur on Cornelia and the sofa, courtesy of the chubby, brown-and-beige cat sprawled across Cornelia's lap. She would have to do some serious lint brushing before any of the wedding party showed up.

The cat looked up at Jillian smugly, then closed his eyes to better enjoy Cornelia's petting. Though Possum was technically Bertie's cat, you'd never know it by his behavior. When Cornelia's husband had died and she'd moved back to Belle Haven to help out with the bills and the gardening on the big estate, it had been love at first sight for Possum. Cornelia was his favorite. Cornelia was certain the affection was because Possum was the incarnation of her late husband, Raymond. Jillian suspected it was because Cornelia constantly snuck treats to the chubby cat.

Suddenly feeling very tired, Jillian reached out to scratch Possum between the eyes. "Why did I ever think event planning was a good idea?"

"Because you are afraid you'll never be a baker," Aunt Cornelia said simply, ignoring her own part in convincing Bertie that The Chocolate Shoppe should expand into larger events held at the mansion. "Which is ridiculous. It's in your blood, and you're getting better all the time; even Bertie says so. You need practice, that's all."

Jillian chose not to jump into a list of her baking failures, spectacular though they were. She *was* getting better. In fact, when she baked at the mansion, the results were almost always completely edible. But she knew her improvements weren't nearly fast enough to gain her grandmother's approval, so she was certain *that* was pure invention on Cornelia's part.

"By the way," Aunt Cornelia said, "the big tub upstairs is draining slowly again."

Jillian groaned. "Is it fast enough to ignore for now or slow enough to grow mosquitoes if we don't get it fixed?"

"Mosquitoes." Cornelia paused, thoughtfully. "You know, it's entirely too bad that nice handyman you hired turned out to be a murderer. If you'd taken a little longer to figure that mystery out, he might have fixed the upstairs plumbing before he went to prison."

"Sorry about that," Jillian said. "The next time I hire a killer, I'll make sure he gets the job done first."

Aunt Cornelia patted her hand. "That's good."

"Aunt Cornelia, I'm not going to hire any more murderers," Jillian said. "I expect we've probably come into contact with all the murderers we'll meet in a lifetime, considering that *ordinary* people never meet any."

Her great-aunt blinked at her. "Yes, dear, but we're Southern. We're born to be *extra*ordinary."

Jillian rubbed at the pain that seemed to form between her eyes when she had these conversations with her aunt. As she rubbed at the tension, she had a thought. "Oh, please close Possum in your room during the wedding, and probably tomorrow night for the rehearsal dinner as well. Alice Blackwater wants her cat in the wedding. It's a big orange tabby, and I don't know how Possum will react to a strange cat in the house."

Her great-aunt turned a fond smile toward the cat in her lap. "Oh, I'm sure it will be fine. Raymond always enjoyed meeting new people. I'm sure you remember that."

"Yes, of course, but just to be safe."

Aunt Cornelia stood, cuddling the big cat in her arms. "Don't worry, dear. I'm sure everything will work out. Raymond would let me know if there was anything to worry about."

Jillian would be happy to avoid any new fanciful pronounce-ments by Raymond. Whatever had made Jillian think she needed to balance remodeling and event planning on top of the demands of the bakery?

Cornelia smiled down at her great-niece. "Do try not to worry so much. I'm going to make a last tour of the gardens. I think we're ready, but it doesn't hurt to be sure."

Jillian nodded before opening the binder on her lap and flipping through the pages. The rehearsal dinner, scheduled two days before the wedding at the family's request, would be the first test of her planning skills. If it went perfectly, she'd finally be able to convince herself she'd made a good decision. She harrumphed at the thought. Since returning to Georgia, when had anything she'd done gone perfectly? She'd be happy if no one turned up dead.

The Thursday morning of the rehearsal dinner dawned bright and beautiful, though Jillian was up well before the sun, rushing around in a near panic as she looked over her list of things that absolutely had to be done.

"Stop fluttering," Bertie commanded when Jillian dashed into the kitchen to count the silverware. Bertie had talked her into using the Belle Haven silver. They had a lot of it, and it was a distinctive pattern. The job of polishing the old silver had almost made Jillian regret agreeing with her grandmother, but as she sorted through the pieces, she had to admit that they looked lovely and elegant.

"Mrs. Blackwater called last night to tell me there will be one extra person at the rehearsal dinner. I have to make sure the poor man actually gets well-polished silverware to eat with," Jillian insisted.

Her grandmother reached out and put her hand on Jillian's. "If the man brings all his neighbors, we'll still have enough silverware. You know full well that we have plenty."

"It never hurts to check."

Bertie sighed and took her hand away.

Jillian returned to sorting the silverware while her grandmother went over her schedule at the bakery. Jillian barely tuned in to her grandmother's words until the end.

"Lenora and I will finish up the chocolate decadence dessert bar and bring it all over as soon as we close up the bakery for the day."

"Early," Jillian squeaked, dropping a handful of silverware. "You're closing early, right?"

"Yes, slightly," Bertie said, crossing the room to peer into the fridge. "Though I do hate to close the door on possible customers."

Jillian pushed down the lurch of panic in her chest. Her grandmother was just pulling her chain. She knew she could count on Bertie and Lenora to have the desserts set up in time. "What do you need from the fridge?"

"I was checking on whether there's enough room for all the food we'll need to put in this evening. Between the dishes the Sweetie Pies are bringing and the desserts from the bakery, it's going to fill up."

Jillian felt a jolt of panic. How had she overlooked the fridge? "Is there enough room?"

Bertie swung the fridge door shut. "Plenty. But thinking about the Sweetie Pies brings me to another important point."

"Which is?"

"I noticed that neither Wanda Jean Maplewood nor Maudie Honeycutt are scheduled to help out tonight or on Saturday. They're long-standing members of the Sweetie Pies, and I'm surprised not to see them on your list."

Jillian gave her grandmother the stink eye. "When were you looking at my list?"

Bertie put her hands on her hips and gave Jillian the stare that always made her spill her guts when she was a teenager. "Don't wander off the topic. Why aren't Wanda Jean and Maudie helping out?"

"Well, Maudie is in her seventies," Jillian said hesitantly. "I can't exactly see her hefting and carrying."

"You do remember that I'm seventy-nine, right?" Bertie asked.

"And you're not hauling tables and carrying trays either," Jillian said. "Though you do have a point, of course. Okay, I admit it. I left them off because they are worse than you and Aunt Cornelia about demanding people answer all sorts of inappropriate questions. This is our first big event, and I don't want our client storming out because Maudie decides to ask her whether she wears a girdle or colors her hair."

"They aren't that bad," Bertie said, though her assertion lacked strength. If Jillian was exaggerating, it wasn't by much. "But this is your event, so you need to handle it how you see fit. Just be prepared for repercussions when Maudie and Wanda Jean figure out that they were excluded."

Jillian watched her grandmother walk out of the kitchen, and an ice-cold ball of doom formed in the pit of her stomach. She pushed the gloom down deeper and glanced toward the fridge, wondering if she should peek inside to be sure there was enough room. No, she was sure that if Bertie said there was enough room, there was. She started out of the room but then ran back and took a quick look before heading for the bakery.

Now she only had to hope that the tables and chairs showed up on time so they could get them into position, and then she could see to it that all the main dinner food was done, and . . . She put a hand to her slightly dizzy head. "It's all going to be fine. It's all going to be fine."

Jillian had just returned from the bakery late in the morning as Savannah Cantrell, with her wavy mahogany-colored hair pulled up into a neat bun, bustled into Belle Haven. A garment bag hung over one arm, a basket from the other, and a big covered Crock-Pot was in her hands. "I knew you were probably having a small panic attack," she said when Jillian greeted her, "so I thought I should show up early."

"You are an angel," Jillian said as she pulled the garment bag from Savannah's arm. "Simply seeing you has already lowered my blood pressure."

Savannah's brown eyes sparkled as she grinned. "That's what friends are for." She hauled the slow cooker into the kitchen and set it on the counter, whipping off the cover to reveal pale dough.

"I made the dough before I left the house, and now it needs to chill. I don't want to do the first rise on the knot rolls until closer to dinnertime. They should be coming out of the oven when the wedding party arrives. There's nothing to beat the smell of fresh yeast rolls for making folks hungry. Plus, I have one other surprise."

"What's that?"

"I had some leftover bread that I'd picked up at the bakery earlier this week, and I made it into something special." Savannah whipped off the cloth covering the basket to reveal heart-shaped croutons, flecked with herbs.

"Those are perfect," Jillian said. "Now you're doubly an angel."

Savannah waved off the compliment. "I sliced the bread and cut the hearts with cookie cutters. Then I buttered the hearts, sprinkled them with herbs, and toasted them in the oven. Easy-peasy."

A phone call kept Jillian from launching into another grateful gush. She stepped over to the quieter breakfast area to take the call and immediately felt her good mood evaporate. The caller was Lilly Quest, the owner of the Quest for Beauty flower shop. The news she had was anything but good.

"I can't have the dinner centerpieces there within the next hour as you expected," Lilly said. "I can have them ready by Friday morning."

"But the rehearsal dinner is tonight," Jillian squeaked. "You know that. Flowers delivered tomorrow morning won't help us with the dinner tonight."

"Your order was very specific and unusual, so I had to make a special order from my wholesaler. The truck carrying all the flowers down from Atlanta was in a wreck. Thankfully, no one was badly injured, but there's nothing I can do about the flowers. I can't exactly drive to the accident site and pick blossoms out of the debris."

Jillian wasn't sure about that. She might be willing to try, but she took a deep breath and spoke as calmly as she could. "How about the actual wedding flowers for Saturday? Will they be delivered tomorrow?"

"There's no problem with those," Lilly said. "They'll be ready by the early afternoon. What do you want to do about the rehearsal centerpieces?"

"Unless you can magically deliver them in the next couple of hours, cancel that order. Everyone is coming tonight; I'll figure something out." Jillian ended the call and fought back the urge to cry. She had no doubt the Blackwaters would be less than thrilled to see bare tables at the rehearsal dinner, no matter how beautiful the delicate Belle Haven china made the tables look.

Savannah put a hand on Jillian's shoulder. "What's wrong?"

Jillian choked out the update on the centerpieces while Savannah listened. Cornelia walked in on the end of the explanation.

"You should have used Rich's Flowers," Cornelia said. "That's the florist Bertie always uses."

"And I would have, but a business card from Quest for Flowers came in the mail with a note from Mrs. Blackwater asking that we use them. I could hardly refuse."

"Of course you couldn't," Savannah said supportively.

"Clearly, there is only one answer for tonight. We will make centerpieces," Cornelia said, putting her hands on her hips in an unconscious imitation of Bertie. "We have some beautiful flowers in bloom, and I've already made several arrangements for the foyer and the living room. Also, I noticed the gardenias are beginning to bloom way back in the areas I haven't tended yet. I didn't use them in the house arrangements, but I think they would be lovely for table displays. They're a bit wild, but they have such a lovely scent that shouldn't be too overwhelming on outdoor tables."

"But what will we put the flowers in?" Jillian asked, still feeling panicky. "And how can we make them suit an *Alice in Wonderland* theme?"

Savannah's face brightened. "*Alice in Wonderland* has the big tea party scene, right? Well, Annalise collects teapots. I've seen them at her house. They're gorgeous. Let me call and have her bring some over. We can make the centerpieces in those."

Cornelia clapped her hands. "That's a marvelous idea. And I have a pack of playing cards in my room. We can scatter cards around the tables in lieu of party confetti."

Jillian looked from her best friend to her aunt. "That could work. You two are geniuses."

"Oh, the big desk in the library has a drawer full of old skeleton keys," Cornelia said. "We could work those into the centerpieces too. As I remember, Alice finds a key to the tiny garden door, remember?"

Jillian did, vaguely, though she suppressed a shudder at going into the mansion's two-story library. It had the potential to be one of the most magnificent rooms in the house, but it would require more money and more time than she had available. So for now, it was musty, shadowy, and more than a little creepy. Still, Jillian was willing to do *anything* to make the centerpieces work.

While Savannah made the call to Annalise, Jillian dashed through the mansion to the library. She hesitated for a moment with her hand on the door, trying to shake off the vague feeling of dread. She'd found the big room spooky as a child, but she was a grown woman now. It was time to give up silly notions about things hiding in the shadows.

She jerked open the door and dashed across the worn Persian rug to the big desk. To her surprise, she saw cat tracks in the dust on the desk. She had no idea that Possum ever went into the neglected room. She pulled open the desk drawer and grabbed the handful of keys. All the while, she had the creepy feeling of being watched, though she knew it was nothing more than her imagination. She slammed the drawer shut and headed back out to the kitchen.

Soon Annalise arrived with a large box full of teapots to choose from in different sizes and shapes. As they arranged them on the breakfast table, Jillian thought they might actually be better centerpieces than the ones she'd ordered from the florist. Annalise also produced a bag stuffed with short lengths of ribbon. "They're left over from various projects," she said. "I'm an incurable pack rat."

"Now we simply need to cut the flowers for the pots," Cornelia said, and she began handing out garden shears and directions for where to find the best flowers.

Savannah saluted playfully before she and Annalise headed out into the front garden with their list of required flowers.

"I'll go cut the gardenias," Cornelia said. "They'll be the focal point of the arrangements, I think."

"Do you want me to come help?" Jillian asked.

Before Cornelia could answer her question, the front doorbell rang, and Jillian ran to answer it, finding that the rented furniture had arrived. She quickly forgot about her aunt as she directed the men about the placement of the tables and chairs in the back garden and explained to them that the extra tables and chairs that wouldn't be needed till the reception should be stored in the garage. She would only use three tables for the rehearsal dinner. She felt that was the perfect number to ensure that each table provided the diners with a view of the well-tended flowers while downplaying the wilder areas farther away. Along with the tables and chairs, the rental service had provided crisp white linen tablecloths and tailored slip covers to disguise the plain metal folding chairs.

She was straightening the drape of one of the tablecloths when she saw her aunt walking toward her from the garden, clutching a basket of gardenia blossoms. Instead of her usual bouncy stride, her great-aunt plodded unevenly, almost staggering. Although always fair, Cornelia's face had turned a sickly, chalk white.

Jillian dropped the edge of the tablecloth and ran to Cornelia's side, gently taking the basket from her and steering her great-aunt toward the nearest chair. "Aunt Cornelia, are you ill? What's wrong?"

"Wrong?" Cornelia echoed, looking up at Jillian.

"You look as if you've seen a ghost."

Cornelia shook her head. "I didn't *see* anything." She turned her eyes back toward the wilder areas of the garden. "But something is out there. I could feel it. I know you and Bertie laugh at my sensitivity to haints, but I sensed something vicious out there, something evil and very, very angry."

Squeezing her aunt's hand, Jillian spoke gently. "The woods are probably full of scurrying animals. I know they make me nervous whenever I wander back there." *Not to mention I was once shot at in those same overgrown gardens.*

Cornelia shook her head. "What I felt was nothing normal or natural." She looked up at Jillian with desperate eyes. "We've made a terrible, terrible mistake in opening the mansion for events. The Belle Haven haint is angry, and I'm afraid we're going to pay for it."

"Pay for it how?" Jillian echoed.

"With death."

Jillian shook off the chill that crept up the back of her neck, raising goose bumps on her skin. "Aunt Cornelia," she said, trying for the no-nonsense tone that Bertie normally used on her eccentric sister, "I'm sure no one is going to die. We're going to have a wedding. It's a happy time, and our guests are going to love the beautiful gardens you've worked so hard on."

"Someone isn't happy about this event," Cornelia whispered.

Jillian almost wept with relief when Savannah and Annalise joined her, holding their baskets of flowers cut from the front garden. "Is something wrong?" Savannah asked.

"Cornelia had a scare in the overgrown land out back," Jillian said. "I think she needs to lie down."

At that, Cornelia seemed to shake off much of her shock. "Of course I don't need to lie down like a fainting Victorian maiden. If you refuse to listen to reason, I can't make you." She stood, wobbling slightly, then pulled herself up very straight. "Ladies, I believe we have some centerpieces to make." She pointed her garden shears at Jillian. "But I won't be coming out here once the dinner begins. I shall make myself useful indoors and hope we don't end up being very sorry by the end of the evening." She straightened her pale floral blouse and squared her shoulders. "Now, let's go!"

"That's the spirit!" Savannah said.

"Don't say 'spirit,'" Jillian whispered, getting a glare from her aunt before Cornelia snatched up the basket of gardenias and marched toward the house. Though she still thought Cornelia looked a bit pale, Jillian had to admit she rallied well, ordering everyone around with gusto.

Since the flower-arranging gene had passed by Jillian with even more enthusiasm than the baking gene, she stood back to watch the magic until she heard her grandmother bellow from the back door.

The chocolates had arrived.

Bertie and Lenora unloaded the desserts onto the polished silver trays lined with delicate paper doilies. Bertie had made gorgeous dark chocolate petits fours, swathed in pastel fondant with tiny royal icing roses and edible rice-paper tags declaring Eat Me! to tie the decoration into the *Alice in Wonderland* theme.

Before leaving the bakery earlier, Jillian had filled and decorated the mini éclairs that served as the second dessert for the decadent chocolate array. As with the petits fours, the tiny éclairs sported royal icing decorations of teacups and flowers. Jillian had become rather good with royal icing and enjoyed turning her natural drawing talents to creating with icing. Bertie had deemed decorating to be one of Jillian's official "safe" duties.

The third desserts were tiny layered white- and dark-chocolate mousse cups. Before serving, each would receive a delicate royal icing playing-card garnish along with a tiny sprig of mint. The individual desserts were small so each guest could indulge in all three if desired, though Jillian felt almost dizzy at the thought of that much rich dessert.

After the mousse cups were stored in the fridge, Lenora got to work on the main dish, consisting of stuffed chicken breast in a delicate sauce. While she worked, Bertie pulled a pot of mock turtle soup from the fridge. At least, they were calling it mock turtle soup. Alice Blackwater had requested mock turtle soup specifically because it was mentioned in *Alice in Wonderland.*

Once they discovered the young woman had never actually tasted mock turtle soup and wasn't at all sure what was in it,

Bertie decided to substitute a nice seafood soup with lots of white wine in it.

"Do you think that's entirely honest?" Jillian had asked at the time.

"I found a recipe for mock turtle soup online," Bertie had answered. "It involves the head of a calf. The whole head. Of a calf. Honestly, Jillian, there was even a step where you scald off the hair. Would you care to do that part?"

Jillian got queasy when she thought about it. After that, she went along with her grandmother's plan cheerfully. The soup warming on the stove smelled delicious, and she didn't want to imagine how Mrs. Blackwater would have responded to the real thing.

Soon, all of the Southern Sweetie Pies were busy whipping up the rehearsal dinner, with the exception of Laura Lee Zane, who hadn't been able to get off work early at the sheriff's office, where she was a deputy. Jillian knew she'd be along to help serve before the first guest arrived, and that was enough.

At one point during the cooking, Cornelia vanished and Jillian wondered if she'd finally given in and gone upstairs to rest. Instead, Cornelia swept back into the kitchen, holding up a handful of pocket watches, dangling from their watch chains. "I just remembered that the White Rabbit carries a pocket watch," she said. "Raymond collected pocket watches, and I'm going to put one on each of the tables in the centerpieces. Raymond's influence should help offset the hostile intent of the haint."

"The haint?" Bertie echocd.

"Aunt Cornelia *felt* something when she was in the back garden," Jillian said. "I think the watches are lovely. And they'll add a lot to the centerpieces."

"They'll add safety," Cornelia insisted. As she left to add the watches to the decorated tables, Jillian heard her grandmother muttering about flaky superstitions.

Laura Lee finally arrived and dashed up to Jillian's room to change into the black slacks and white blouse that would mark her as a server once the rehearsal was over and dinner began. Lenora and Savannah followed suit.

For her role as hostess, Jillian had chosen a simply tailored, sage-green linen dress. Bertie wore her normal bakery whites with a plain apron. Since Cornelia had no intention of serving, she wore a frilly apron over her usual floral dress.

As the early evening shadows were darkening the woods, the wedding party began to show up, and Jillian was pleased to see them admiring the old mansion. The wedding rehearsal was as close to flawless as anyone could hope. The bridesmaids muttered to one another about the dresses they would wear on Saturday. The mother of the bride glared daggers at her husband, her daughter, the mother of the groom, and most anyone else who got too close to her. The bride's cat yowled constantly from the carrier, making it difficult for everyone to hear directions from the soft-spoken pastor. And the groom showed up late, which meant he had to be scolded by everyone before the rehearsal could begin. Even so, Jillian was pleased as she watched the proceedings. It all looked like a very normal wedding rehearsal.

A golden glow from the lights of the front veranda spilled out onto the front garden, where the wedding was to be held. The garden was beautiful with azaleas bursting with salmon, white, and pink, and pansies still filled the low beds with their happy faces. Jillian had been lavish in the placement of solar lights in the beds, which helped with safety and with highlighting the beauty of the area.

The flowering trees brought the color up around the wedding party, and Jillian had strung them with white battery-operated twinkle lights to help brighten the early evening shadows during the rehearsal. The eastern redbuds were especially gorgeous with their pink double blooms that matched the delicate color of the speckled lilies nodding in the beds below them. The natural floral perfume sweetened the soft evening breeze. With so much blooming, the flowers that would arrive on Saturday seemed almost unnecessary.

When the rehearsal ended, Jillian put on her most welcoming smile. "If you will all follow me, I'll lead you to the rehearsal dinner in the back gardens."

"These gardens are positively magical," Mrs. Liddell gushed as she stepped up to walk beside Jillian. The slender woman had a bent, beaky nose and a bright, inquisitive look. "You'd better be careful or I'll steal away your gardener."

Jillian smiled at her. "Since my great-aunt is the artist behind our gardens, I think I'm safe from anyone luring her away from home."

They walked through the front door of Belle Haven and into the large foyer with the beautiful, polished wooden floors. On tables along the walls, vases filled with flowers brought their sweet scent into the house, a marked improvement over the smell of fresh paint that had greeted Jillian for quite some time after remodeling began.

To the left of the foyer, the French doors to the formal dining room were closed. She'd considered having the rehearsal dinner in the dining room at the long table, but it would have been tight with all the attendants Alice Blackwater had chosen. The back garden offered much more room.

As they passed the elegant curving stairway, Mrs. Liddell looked up and gasped at the huge stained glass dome far above. During the day, the dome flooded the stairs with golden light. In the evening, newly installed lighting pointed upward to draw attention to the amazing workmanship of the stained glass. "How lovely," the older woman breathed.

"Thank you," Jillian said, wincing as she remembered how much it had cost to get someone onto the roof to clean the dome. Not surprisingly, none of the Sweetie Pies had volunteered for *that* job.

They walked through the living room and out onto the back veranda. From there, they could see the tables with their crisp white linen cloths and unique centerpieces. Alice Blackwater squealed with delight as soon as she saw them. "Teapots!" she said. "How wonderful. They're absolutely perfect." She held up the cat carrier and cooed at the complaining cat inside. "Aren't they perfect, Chess?"

No sign of agreement came from the cat.

"At least they're tasteful," Mrs. Blackwater muttered as she swept by Jillian.

During the remodel, a section of the back-garden plants had simply been pulled out and sod laid down to allow a larger lawn for events. Where the tables were set up, a kind of outdoor-room effect was created, with paving stones and wrought-iron trellises that bounded the space and led the eye into the flower gardens beyond. More solar lights lined the path to the table area, and the bright days they'd enjoyed all week meant the solar lights all shone beautifully in the early evening.

The carefully tended area of back garden was still fairly small, and the trees beyond loomed tall enough to bring considerable shadows to the garden even with the lengthening spring days. Jillian had strung more white lights on all the trellises. Electric candles mixed in with the centerpieces gave the area a soft, magical look.

After more compliments on the decorating, the wedding party slowly took their seats, and dinner began with the mock, mock turtle soup. Laura Lee and Savannah carried silver trays loaded with small white crocks of soup and spoons. They each grinned at Jillian as they passed, then began serving the guests with perfect professionalism. Jillian felt a fresh flood of appreciation for the kindness of the Sweetie Pies in making the dinner work. Thankfully, no one in the party pointed out that seafood bisque and mock turtle soup were radically different foods. Instead, they complimented the soup lavishly.

Next, her friends brought out a light garden salad made from the greens Jillian had picked up only that morning at a local farm. The farmer had mixed the normal baby field greens with edible flowers, which gave the salads a unique taste and look. Along with the greens, Savannah's heart-shaped croutons and Jillian's freshly made raspberry vinaigrette completed the appealing salad course.

Jillian had to stifle a chuckle. She'd finally gotten a salad onto a Chocolate Shoppe menu, something Bertie had frequently vetoed.

Though light conversation continued, Jillian found that the sniping had vanished. *The power of good food prevails*, she thought with a smile. *Now, if we can only keep everyone happy through the main course and dessert.* She really didn't have much doubt that they would remain content after having smelled and seen everything in the kitchen herself.

Laura Lee swept by again with a pitcher of sweet tea, a white tea towel wrapped around the pitcher to keep the condensation from dripping on guests as she poured. She winked at Jillian as she walked by. When she'd first met Laura Lee Zane, Jillian hadn't imagined becoming friends with the young sheriff's deputy. Of course, Jillian had been miffed about being accused of murder at the time, so her judgment may have been a bit faulty. Still, she now considered the lighthearted young woman to be one of her best friends in Moss Hollow, second only to Savannah, and was glad Laura Lee was part of the Sweetie Pies.

After topping off glasses, Laura Lee walked over to stand by Jillian. "Everything seems to be going well."

Jillian nodded, almost nervous at the thought of agreeing as if that might jinx everything. "I should make Bertie come out and watch people eating salads."

Laura Lee grinned. "Your grandmother will never see salad as real food. She once told me that it's something you eat as penance to assuage your guilt about chocolate."

"That's about right," Jillian said; then her attention was drawn by movement from the corner of her eye. She looked back toward the shadowy garden. Had something moved in the shadows? "Do you see anything in the garden?"

"You mean like a possum?" Laura Lee asked, peeking around Jillian to peer in the same direction.

"Bigger."

Jillian's rapt stare began to draw the attention of the guests at the tables. At the sound of movement in the deep brush, Jillian walked closer to the nearest trellis, peering past it and into the garden. Where the garden was clipped and weeded back into its proper order, everything seemed still, but something was definitely moving through the trees along one edge. "It might be a deer," Jillian said softly, as much to herself as to Laura Lee.

"You think?" Laura Lee stepped around Jillian and walked past the trellis. "It would be an unusually brave deer to come this close to a place with so many people outside."

Jillian heard chairs moving and turned to see several of the guests standing up to look in the direction of the garden. She instantly felt guilty. Why had she let something rustling in the brush intrude on her guests' dinner? She stepped back from the trellis, turning completely to face her guests with a smile. "I'm sure it's only a deer. Nothing to worry about."

"You don't have bears or mountain lions out here, do you?" Alice asked nervously, scooting her chair back to stand and pick up the cat carrier from where it rested on the ground next to her chair.

"No," Jillian said with a smile. "We rarely even see deer. These are more of a possum-and-raccoon type of woods, and they won't come out into the light with so many people here. Really, I'm sure it's nothing."

Alice didn't seem to hear her. Instead, she looked past Jillian, and the color drained from her face at an alarming rate. She pointed past Jillian with a shaking hand.

Jillian spun to find Laura Lee clutching the metal trellis as she stared at the border of the woods where a slightly built man stood. The man was covered in mud, tattered clothing, and something resembling swamp slime. It slid down his face, obscuring his features, but he never reached up to wipe it away. Instead, he seemed to mimic Alice's movement, pointing at her. His mouth opened wide and water gushed out. Then the man spoke in a rough, gargling voice. "Alice."

The sound of his voice broke the spell over the frozen group. Alice screamed, jerking Jillian's attention back to the guest tables. The young woman's eyes rolled up, and she slumped in a faint, dropping the cat carrier. As soon as it hit the ground, the door sprang open, and the Cheshire Cat wannabe leapt out into the darkness, racing toward the dark garden and the looming figure. The spooky intruder howled, but Alice still held Jillian's attention as she rushed toward the fainting young woman, though she knew she was too far away to reach her before she collapsed.

Alice would have hit the ground if she hadn't been caught in the arms of her fiancé. With Alice safely in Gordon's arms, Jillian turned her attention from her guests to the muddy intruder, only to discover that he had vanished. All she saw was Laura Lee racing through the garden, then into the woods where the man had disappeared.

With the young deputy on the intruder's trail, Jillian turned her attention to her guests. "Let me help you get her into the house," she said.

"What was that?" Mrs. Blackwater demanded.

Her daughter seemed to rally slightly, turning to look in the direction of the woods, even as her fiancé helped her walk. "It was Jacob," she whispered. "I know it was Jacob."

"Jacob?" Jillian echoed.

"Jacob Zimmer," Gordon Liddell said, his own face pale in the shadowy garden light. "He was my best friend."

"Was?" Jillian said, wondering at the strange prank Gordon's ex-best friend had played.

Gordon blinked at her, his pale eyes slightly unfocused. "He's dead. Jacob Zimmer is dead."

The wedding party trooped into the living room of Belle Haven, and Gordon lowered Alice carefully onto one of the long sofas. The young woman shuddered, turning her face back toward the windows that lined the wall and looked out over the garden. "Where is Jacob?" she asked.

Gordon cleared his throat, seeming to pull himself together after the shock. "I don't know who that was," he said, "but it couldn't have been Jacob. You know it couldn't." He lowered his voice, his tone turning gentle. "Jacob is dead, Alice. You know that."

She blinked at him. "They never found his body. Maybe he's been looking for me all this time. Maybe he found his way back."

Jillian's gaze flashed from person to person in the group, hoping someone would explain exactly what they were talking about. She was desperate to know, but it wasn't her place to ask those kinds of personal questions.

Mrs. Blackwater took a step closer to her daughter. "Don't be ridiculous. He certainly wouldn't turn up at your rehearsal dinner covered in ooze. This was clearly someone's idea of a sick joke." She turned her glare toward Jillian. "I blame you for this. What kind of security do you people have?"

"This is a private home," Jillian said. "I don't hire security guards for a rehearsal dinner. I hardly expected this kind of experience."

The mayor stepped closer and laid a hand on his wife's arm. "I don't see any way this could be Miss Green's fault,

Mary. This was clearly a practical joke someone is playing at Gordon's expense."

"Unless it's a sick joke at Alice's expense," Mrs. Liddell said defensively. "Jacob Zimmer was my son's friend, but he was your daughter's fiancé!"

"I'm not sure there is anything to be gained by placing blame," Jillian said, desperate to calm things before they spiraled completely out of hand.

"Why is everyone inside?" Bertie bellowed across the room. "The main course is ready to be served."

"We had a problem outside," Jillian said. "I'm not sure our guests will want to go back out to the garden."

"No," Alice said, her voice shaky. "Not back out there."

"We can set up in the dining room," Jillian said, desperately glad that the dining room was one of the recently remodeled spaces. In fact, it was the most recently painted; she hoped the smell of paint didn't linger too badly. "Let me get everyone a drink to sip in here while we set up."

Jillian quickly sent Savannah out to the garage for one of the smaller rented tables to augment the seating available at the long dining room table. The small table would hold a chocolate fountain at the wedding reception, but for the moment, it would help prevent everyone from being squished together.

Lenora retrieved a few of the chairs from outdoors. They soon had everyone seated and enjoying the main course, or rather, enjoying it as much as possible directly after seeing a slime-covered dead man walk out of the woods.

Jillian had to give the wedding party credit. They certainly tried very hard to put the ugly business in the garden behind them, and the rest of the rehearsal dinner was almost normal. Jillian did notice, however, that Alice was extremely quiet and barely touched her dinner. The rolling chocolate cart was especially successful. Apparently even a ghoul couldn't kill a love for fine chocolate.

Jillian had to focus on the needs of the guests, but she couldn't help but notice that Laura Lee was still missing, and she found herself increasingly nervous about it. As Bertie rolled out the dessert cart and launched into a description of each offering, Jillian slipped back into the kitchen.

"Has anyone seen Laura Lee?"

With both arms in a sink full of dishes and soap suds, Savannah turned worried eyes toward her and shook her head. "She's a trained deputy," she said. "Surely she'll be all right."

Lenora paused on her way out of the kitchen with a pitcher of tea. "She's also stubborn. She's been that way since she was a little girl in my Sunday school class. If she's after that spook, she won't give up easily."

"I'd feel better if she was back here," Jillian said.

Lenora reached out to pat Jillian's arm with a damp hand. "She'll be fine."

Jillian nodded at the tall woman, and Lenora walked out to the dining room with the tea.

Savannah turned from the sink, drying her hands off on a towel. "Do you think we should go looking for her?"

"I'm not exactly the woodsy type," Jillian said. "Especially in the dark. I'm not sure I could do much more than get lost."

"I have to admit, I usually stick to nice well-tended paths myself," Savannah said.

"You two will stay right here," Bertie announced as she walked back into the kitchen. "Otherwise, we'll have to send Laura Lee out to find the both of you after she gets back. That young woman is extremely capable. She'll be along directly, dragging that fake spook by the scruff of the neck."

Bertie's prediction proved to be half right. When the rehearsal dinner was finishing up, Jillian stole a moment to peer through the tall windows at the end of the breakfast nook and caught sight of Laura Lee heading toward the house from the back garden. "There she is!"

"Good," Bertie said. "We can use some help cleaning up."

Jillian gave her grandmother a sharp look and headed toward the living room where doors led outside. Bertie called out to her. "Get Laura Lee's story later. You still have guests."

With a sigh, Jillian nodded and returned to the dining room. As she walked into the room, the bride-to-be rallied slightly and called out, "Where is Chess? I left the carrier outside. I have to get Chess!"

She stood abruptly, and her fiancé popped up beside her. "Alice, darling, you dropped the cat box outside. The door sprang open, and Chess ran off."

Alice's eyes widened. "No, I have to go find her!" She tried to shrug off her fiancé, but he kept hold of her arm.

"You don't want to go back out there in the dark," he said. "I'm sure Chess will come back once she's calmed down."

"Yes, don't be foolish," Mrs. Blackwater snapped. "You have guests."

"I'll go look for Chess," Jillian said. "Does she have a favorite food? Maybe we can tempt her back."

"She loves fish," Alice said weakly, allowing Gordon to coax her back into her chair.

Jillian scooped a little bit of her grandmother's fish chowder into a shallow bowl and carried it outside. She called for the cat repeatedly but got no response. With a sigh, she set the bowl down next to one of the trellises and went back inside to convey the bad news to the bride-to-be.

The wedding party was finishing up the toasts as she slipped back into the dining room to stand near the door.

When the toasts were done, Jillian stepped up to whisper to

Alice. "I wasn't able to find Chess, but I will keep looking. We have cat carriers here, so when we find her, we'll hold on to her and make sure you get her back."

"All right," Alice whispered, though she looked far from happy.

Jillian read her list of last-minute reminders for the wedding party to follow on Saturday, then the party slowly broke up. Mrs. Blackwater swept by Jillian with barely a nod, but her husband stopped. The mayor was a big man, easily a match for his tall wife. He nearly filled the doorway as he paused to smile brightly at Jillian, his nose and cheeks rather flushed from the dessert champagne he'd generously indulged in during the toasts. "Despite that rather rude joke one of the children's friends seems to have made, I thought the evening was lovely. You're doing a fine job, Miss Green."

Jillian returned his smile. "Thank you. I'm glad everyone enjoyed themselves."

He nodded. "They did. Even my wife, though she'd never admit it. I do hope you find Alice's silly cat. It's a horrible beast, but she's fond of it." He sighed deeply. "It's hard to believe my little girl is getting married, especially after the terrible business with her last fiancé. To be honest, I always preferred Jacob to Gordon, but for all that, Jacob had odd hobbies. Neither boy is really an appropriate match for my little girl, but I hate to argue with the women in my life. Sometimes you have to do what's best for everyone. And Gordon was the last man standing, you know?"

Curiosity urged Jillian to ask about Jacob's odd hobbies, but she knew better than to gossip with clients. Besides, the mayor wasn't making a lot of sense, so instead, she simply said, "I'm sure Alice will be very happy."

The mayor nodded solemnly. "I know I've done everything

I could to make that happen." Then he excused himself to walk out in search of his wife.

With the doorway clear, Jillian was able to see who had been standing behind the mayor. It was Gordon Liddell, who glared at the mayor's broad back, slipping through the door without even a nod toward Jillian.

When the last guest had left, Jillian hurried back to the kitchen. She found Laura Lee sitting in the breakfast nook, sipping sweet tea. "Bertie wouldn't let me work," Laura Lee complained with a wry smile. "She said I look like something the cat dragged in."

"You look like someone who spent over an hour crashing through the woods," Jillian said, slipping into a chair across from her friend. "Though I wouldn't have minded if you'd dragged a cat back in with you. Chess escaped."

Laura Lee took a long sip of the tea. "Sorry, I didn't see a cat."

"Did you see the guy who played ghost?" Jillian asked.

Laura Lee set the damp glass down on the breakfast table, shaking her head. "I only caught glimpses of his back. Whoever he was, that guy can run."

"Ghosts often move with unnatural speed," Cornelia said as she drifted over from the kitchen area. "I'm certain the specter is the angry presence I felt earlier in the garden."

"You may have sensed the guy, I suppose," Laura Lee said, "but he was no ghost. He left clumps of muddy Spanish moss on brush and branches as he passed."

"That isn't proof," Cornelia said. "Drowned ghosts often leave puddles behind after a manifestation."

"If he was a ghost, why not simply vanish?" Laura Lee asked. "I chased that guy for over a mile before he gave me the slip."

"Perhaps he was leading you somewhere," Cornelia said. "Ghosts often lead the living to their final resting place."

"When did you become an expert on ghosts?" Bertie demanded, crossing her arms over her chest. "Have you been watching those crazy TV shows with the fools scaring each other half to death in dark buildings?"

Cornelia sniffed. "I believe it's important to be informed about these things, considering we have a ghost right in this house."

Bertie shook her head. "An imaginary ghost."

"The Belle Haven haint is a well-documented phenomenon," Cornelia said.

"Meaning it turns up in journals by the flakier members of our family," Bertie said. "I've lived in this house all my life, and the only spooky thing I've seen in it is you!"

Jillian reached up to rub her forehead, where a headache was gathering again. "The family seemed to think this was someone's idea of a crude prank, and I believe that's a reasonable theory."

Bertie looked pleased at Jillian's dismissal of the ghost idea, but Cornelia shook her head sadly. "You're becoming as linear and close-minded as my sister. It's quite a disappointment actually." She lifted her head and walked back to the kitchen, where she picked up a linen dish towel and began polishing the silver. Bertie walked back to the kitchen as well to spoon the leftover soup into a large container for the fridge.

"I appreciate you going after the guy," Jillian said, turning back to Laura Lee. "If nothing else, you kept him from trying another stunt at the dinner."

"If this is something more than a passing joke, you might want to keep an eye out on Saturday," the young deputy said, frowning slightly. "If someone is trying to stop the wedding, you could have another manifestation then."

"That's a charming thought," Jillian said with a groan, standing back up. "Well, to paraphrase Scarlett O'Hara, I'll worry about that tomorrow. For tonight, I'm going to help clean up."

"Me too," Laura Lee said. "I've had enough recovery time."

"Are you sure? You've gone above and beyond the call. It's all right if you want to call it a night and go home," Jillian said.

Laura Lee gave her usual saucy grin. "Naw, I better stick around in case y'all get haunted again during the cleanup."

Luckily, they saw no more ghostly activity for the rest of the evening. Jillian shared all the compliments she'd gotten on the food and service while they worked. Finally, the kitchen and dining room were back to their usual immaculate standard, and the rented tables were folded and lined up along one wall in the breakfast nook.

"You all should head on home," Jillian told her friends as she laid the pile of linen chair covers on the breakfast nook table. The covers were trimmed with pale-pink ribbons, and Jillian needed to check them all over for possible stains. "I can bring in the folding chairs, and then I'll head up to bed."

Her grandmother and aunt had already gone upstairs to bed before the younger women tackled the tables, and Jillian felt guilty about keeping her friends for so long.

"No argument from me," Lenora said. "I've been up since before the sun, and my feet are tired of me standing on them. Will you be at the bakery tomorrow?"

"In the morning," Jillian said. "I need to be home when the flowers are delivered right after lunch."

"I'll see you then." Lenora gave her a hug, then grabbed her things and headed out.

"You sure you don't want us to help with the chairs?" Savannah asked as she and Laura Lee gathered their things.

Jillian couldn't miss how tired her friend sounded. "No, you both go on. I want to take a last look around, and I can think better when I'm alone. Besides, you two need your recovery time since we're going to do this all again for the reception on Saturday, only about three times bigger."

"That would be terrifying if I thought about it very long," Savannah said. She gave Jillian a one-armed hug, then she and Laura Lee left.

Jillian walked out to the garden and began folding the chairs, leaning them against one of the trellises until she was ready to carry them into the house. As she worked, her gaze kept drifting to the back garden. She knew it was unlikely the intruder would come back. He couldn't possibly expect the bridal party to be at the house so late, but she couldn't shake off the nervous feeling that someone was out there watching her.

"Great," she muttered to herself. "I'm turning into Cornelia in my old age."

Finally, all of the chairs leaned against the trellis. Jillian decided to face her silly nerves and marched through the trellis to the garden paths beyond.

She hadn't bought enough solar lights to illuminate the paths that wound between the garden beds, but the moon was only two days from being full, and with the cloudless sky, it offered her considerable light. She wasn't in danger of falling over the low garden beds or tripping on any of the tree roots that snaked in from the woods beyond.

She looked around and realized that the intruder could have left all kinds of clues; she simply didn't have enough light to see them. With a sigh, she stopped at the edge of the woods, staring into the darkness that even the moon couldn't penetrate.

As she looked, her imagination conjured up all kinds of ghouls staring back at her, and she felt goose bumps raise on her arms. "Oh, I'm being an idiot," she scolded herself. Just as she spoke, something soft brushed against the back of her legs, making her jump with a shriek.

Something shrieked back at her as she landed on the creature's paw. Jillian caught only a glimpse, but she immediately recognized Chess racing away from her, back toward the house. "Hold on there," Jillian called, dashing after the cat and hoping the angry animal didn't disappear.

Apparently, Chess had had enough adventure for one night because she sat next to the back door and meowed plaintively until Jillian reached her. "Good kitty, Chess," Jillian Said. "Alice will be glad to know you're recovered!" She scooped the cat up and carried it inside.

She didn't want to wake her aunt by looking for the cat carrier that Cornelia kept in her room, so Jillian simply shut Chess up in the laundry room with a bowl of fresh water and a shallow cardboard box of cat litter. "Sorry for the accom- modations," she told the big tabby, "but we weren't expecting overnight guests."

Chess merely curled up in the laundry basket where Jillian had tossed some old towels and closed her eyes.

"I know how you feel," Jillian said. Then she closed the door and headed back outside to grab the chairs. She made it a point to stand up straight while marching out, not giving place to any more nerves. It was time to stop being a silly goose and get the job done.

Friday morning began with Jillian's alarm clock attempting to drill a hole in her skull. At least, that's the way it felt. She sat up in bed, rubbing at the headache she seemed to have kept from the night before. She staggered to the bathroom and peered into the mirror, horrified to discover that her tangled hair looked positively feral. She shuffled into the shower, hoping to drown the mess on her head.

By the time she got downstairs, Bertie and Cornelia were finishing up a breakfast of warmed-up rolls left over from the rehearsal dinner. As soon as Jillian walked into the room, Cornelia slathered a roll with butter and jam and handed it to Jillian. "What time did you get to bed last night?"

"Late," Jillian grumbled. She flopped into a chair, dropped the roll onto a saucer, and poured herself a cup of coffee from the pot on the table. "Along with bringing in the rented furniture, I had to make a guest room for Chess. She nearly gave me a heart attack in the garden, but at least we've recovered her. I sent Alice an e-mail about it before I went to bed. She's coming by the bakery later to pick her up."

"You're bringing an animal to the bakery?" Bertie asked, clearly not in favor of the idea.

"In the carrier," Jillian said.

"It's still an animal," Bertie said. "In the bakery. A place where we make food."

"It's our client's pet," Jillian said. "A client who hasn't paid all the bills yet. And she won't do anymore harm to the bakery than she did to me last night. She nearly gave me a coronary, sneaking up on me in the garden."

"I imagine Chess was probably trying to protect you from the specter," Cornelia said as she wiped delicately at her fingers with the napkin. "Even ordinary cats are quite sensitive to spirits. She probably wanted to warn you about the specter's presence."

"I'm not sure scaring me half to death was all that helpful."

"It's your own reluctance to embrace extreme possibilities that scares you."

"I'm pretty sure it was having something rub against my leg in the dark." Jillian took a big bite of the roll and found it was as perfectly tender and flaky as it had been the night before.

"If the two of you are done," Bertie said, "I have something to say that is not on the topic of haints and horrors." She pointed at Jillian. "How early are you planning to come in to the bakery this morning?"

"I'm not sure. I'll have to get the carrier for the cat, but I can leave with you, I suppose," Jillian said. "Though if you're planning an elaborate baking lesson, I'm not sure I've had enough sleep, so you can't blame me if something goes up in flames."

"You're entirely too negative about your baking," Bertie said, which made Jillian gape at her. Her grandmother had not hesitated to be negative about Jillian's efforts on previous occasions. "You come from a long line of magnificent cooks and bakers, and you have already shown competence in pastry decoration."

"Um, thanks?" Jillian said, still nervously waiting for the part where Bertie yelled at her for something.

"You're welcome," Bertie said simply, then drank down the rest of the coffee in her cup. "I'm leaving for the bakery, but you don't need to come now. You should eat a good breakfast before you do. And be sure Chess is secure in the cat carrier, which should stay near the back door or maybe under the apartment stairs near the side door."

"I promise I won't let the cat run around the bakery," Jillian said.

"I should hope not," Bertie said. "We have enough problems without a health code violation." She stood and brushed crumbs from the front of her shirt. "I believe Lenora will be working with you on decorating the wedding cake."

Jillian's eyes opened wide. "The wedding cake?" she squeaked. "I don't think we should risk my messing that up."

"You won't mess it up," Bertie said, making the reassurance sound more like a command. "Lenora says you're quite talented. Follow her lead, and it will be fine."

Jillian swallowed the knot in her throat as she watched her grandmother stride across the room. Her first wedding cake would also be for her first event client. What could go wrong?

"You'll be fine."

Jillian jumped at the sound of her great-aunt's voice. She'd been sitting so quietly at the breakfast table that Jillian had forgotten she was there. "Thanks, Aunt Cornelia. By the way, are you going to be around all morning?"

Her aunt nodded as she dabbed at her lips with a napkin. "Do you need me for some pre-wedding activity?"

"Not exactly," Jillian said. "Harold Johnson is coming over this morning with a small crew to build the stage area for the band. He knows where it should be located, and he's bringing the tools and wood. Really, you won't need to do anything since they'll be outside, but if it's hot, you may want to bring them some lemonade."

"You're not putting the stage too close to where the specter appeared, are you?" Cornelia asked in alarm. "I don't think it's wise to anger the haint again."

"No, I'm sure it'll be in a specter-safe area."

"Good." Cornelia stood and began clearing the small table. "I will make certain none of the men die from heat exhaustion."

As soon as Jillian arrived at the bakery, Lenora insisted that it wasn't fair for the poor cat to spend all morning in the cat carrier, so she insisted on toting Chess down to the library. "Josi Rosenschein loves cats, and she can keep her in the staff room where the little darlin' can have more room."

Jillian wasn't certain the cat was either little or darling, but if the kindhearted librarian was willing to look after the furry monster, Jillian certainly wouldn't argue. "As long as that cat doesn't run off. We're having enough drama with this wedding as it is."

"You worry too much," Lenora said as she bustled through the back door, hauling the heavy carrier as if it weighed no more than a purse.

As the door swung shut, Jillian marveled that she hadn't gotten ulcers from the quiet country life she'd experienced since coming back to Georgia. With a sigh, she pulled on a fresh pink hairnet and faced the day.

Jillian had finished setting out the supplies they would need for decorating by the time Lenora returned empty-handed. Before Jillian could speak, Lenora held up her hand. "Josi promised not to let the cat disappear again. Now, let me wash my hands and we'll get to work."

Lenora was endlessly patient as she walked Jillian through the creation of the decorations for the cake. When Jillian had originally booked the event, she and Lenora has spent hours designing the cake. Together, they had looked at dozens of images of *Alice in Wonderland* wedding cakes online. Most would have sent Mrs. Blackwater into a rage, with their tilted levels and brightly colored decorations. In the end, they'd settled on a cake with white frosting and decorations that combined roses, lace, pocket watches, and delicate teacups made from royal icing and gum paste.

For the teacup molds, they had used a darling set of miniature china teacups that Jillian bought at The Dusty Magnolia, an antique shop in the middle of town. Thankfully, they'd cast way more teacups than they needed, because assembling them resulted in some breakage. Jillian looked woefully at the broken teacup in her hands. She'd accidentally pushed her finger through the side while putting on the handle.

"Don't you mind that a bit," Lenora said. "We'll cut that one in half and use the unbroken side."

Jillian nodded and gently set the cup down to shake out the tension in her hands. She looked at her grandmother's oldest friend for a moment, then said, "I don't think I've ever thanked you for staying on at the bakery."

Lenora looked at her in surprise, her brown eyes wide. "Staying on? Why wouldn't I stay on?"

"Bertie told me you moved into the apartment upstairs temporarily," Jillian said, and Lenora nodded. "She said you were staying there until I got good enough to take over the bakery. Then you wanted to move to Alabama to be with your grandbaby. I know I'm taking a long time to get good—" She stopped abruptly when Lenora burst out laughing. "I don't get the joke."

Lenora put down the piping bag she'd been using. "I sold my house so I could help out my daughter with college tuition so she could go back to school, but I didn't ever intend to go to Alabama for more than a few days at a time. I love my daughter and my grandbaby to the moon and back again, but life is a lot calmer if we don't live too close together. My daughter is so strong-willed, she ought to be Bertie's young'un."

"But Bertie said—"

"I was planning to rent a trailer in Aunt Venus's park," Lenora said. "But your grandmother offered the apartment, and it's convenient." She smiled at Jillian. "I really think she wanted the apartment in use so you couldn't sneak up there and avoid living at the mansion with her and Cornelia. At any rate, I'm perfectly happy, though I wouldn't mind a new air conditioner. I expect I'll move closer to my grandbaby someday, and probably said as much, but I'm happy for now."

Jillian wasn't quite sure what to say to that revelation, but she was spared having to figure it out when she heard her name called.

Maggie, the most recent front girl Bertie had hired after the last one left to be a full-time mom to her new baby, poked her head around the doorway that led out front. "A Miss Blackwater wants to talk to you."

Jillian jumped up, bumping the table, but thankfully not creating any breakage. "Sorry," she said to Lenora. "I'll be right back."

Lenora offered her a big smile. "No problem. Take as long as you need. We're making good time."

Jillian looked over the scattering of tiny cups and roses, and hoped that was true.

She hung her apron on the hook next to the doorway and slipped off her hairnet as she passed into the front of the bakery. She spotted Alice Blackwater right away, sitting in one of the bistro chairs and picking at her manicure nervously.

Crossing the room quickly, Jillian pasted on her best smile. "I know you've been worried about Chess, but she's fine. She's down at the library. I'll walk down with you."

"Thank you," Alice said softly. From the dark circles under the young woman's eyes, Jillian assumed she'd not slept well after the rehearsal dinner, so she was glad to assuage her worries about the cat. Her joy was short-lived when the woman spoke up tensely. "Actually, I need your help with something else."

"Oh?"

"You have to help me find Jacob," Alice said, turning shadowed eyes toward Jillian. "Dead or alive."

"You want me to look for your former fiancé?" Jillian said, dropping her voice to a fierce whisper as she settled into the chair across from Alice Blackwater. "You do know I'm only a baker and an event planner, not a detective or a police officer."

"The police already looked for him and found absolutely nothing helpful," Alice said, leaning across the table toward Jillian. "And I heard about you. You're smart. I heard how you figured out who killed Nadine Belmont and Otis Dupree. Now I want you to figure this out too."

"You do realize there was a lot of luck involved in both of those events you named and not all of it good," Jillian said. "There is no reason to believe I would do any better than the police."

"Fine, you figured those things out because you're lucky. I'm okay with that. Maybe luck will help." Alice wrapped her arms around herself, and tears filled her eyes. "I have to know what happened to Jacob. If he is dead, I need to know. If he's alive and mad about my marrying Gordon, I want to know. Either way, I don't want him haunting me for the rest of my life."

"I honestly do not believe that a ghost showed up at your rehearsal dinner," Jillian said. "Whoever that was, he left behind mud and moss."

"Fine. Then Jacob is alive. In that case, I want to talk to him."

"I'm not sure that you should jump to that conclusion. Maybe someone is playing a cruel joke at your fiancé's expense. You did say Jacob was Gordon's friend."

"If that's the case, then I want to know that too." Alice raised her chin stubbornly. "But I don't believe this is a joke.

I recognized that figure. It was Jacob. I would certainly know my own fiancé."

"It was dark," Jillian said gently. "The man was very muddy. And shock can play tricks on you."

"It was Jacob. I want to know what happened to him. Where's he been? Why did he disappear? And why scare me like that?" Her voice hitched into a sob. "I thought he loved me."

Alarmed, Jillian reached out and patted her client's arm. "I'm sure he did."

Alice looked at Jillian with wide, watery eyes. "Will you help? Will you find out what happened to Jacob?"

"I honestly have no idea how I can help," Jillian said. "Have you talked about this with your fiancé?"

Alice sighed. "Not really. Gordon went off today on some last hurrah with a few of his friends." She smiled slightly. "I was a little surprised he was willing to go, to be honest. He normally won't miss work for anything."

Eager to turn the conversation away from the search for Jacob, Jillian jumped on the new topic. "What does Gordon do for a living?"

"He works for the town, as a clerk." She smiled slightly. "That's actually how Gordon and Jacob met. Jacob wanted to do some remodeling at his antique shop and needed permits. Gordon handled the permits, and they hit it off."

"So they didn't know each other long," Jillian said.

Alice shook her head. "Only about a year before Jacob disappeared." She drooped visibly in her chair and looked toward the big front window of the bakery. "I wish I'd asked Gordon not to go off today, but he said it would make our marriage that much luckier, since he was sure not to see the bride before the wedding. That sounded fine before Jacob showed up. Now, I wish I had Gordon here."

"If Gordon isn't worried about the sick prank last night, maybe he has an idea who did it," Jillian suggested. "I'm sure he wouldn't have left you alone if he thought you were in danger."

"No, I don't suppose he would."

"Look, let's go get Chess. I know she's missed you. Then you should concentrate on tomorrow and your wedding, and put last night out of your mind."

The younger woman looked at her sadly. "I guess." She sniffled and blinked her eyes rapidly. "You're right. I should concentrate on the wedding. Gordon loves me, and we're going to have a whole life together."

"That's the right attitude!" Jillian said. Alice dabbed at her eyes with a tissue from her purse; then she stood up and squared her shoulders. Jillian herded Alice gently out of the bakery and down the street to the library.

After a touching reunion between Alice and Chess, Jillian gratefully sent the young woman on her way and headed back to the bakery to finish working on the cake. Instead, she found Mrs. Blackwater standing in the middle of the customer area of the bakery, trying vainly to stare down Bertie. All around the room, customers sat at the little bistro tables watching the two women in rapt fascination. There's nothing Moss Hollow enjoyed more than a good drama.

Bertie caught sight of Jillian. "Mrs. Blackwater stopped by while you were out gadding about."

Jillian ignored her grandmother's jab and smiled up at the mayor's wife. "Mrs. Blackwater, I'm so sorry for the unpleasantness last night."

"Unpleasantness you should have prevented!"

"High jinks by friends of the wedding party are not our responsibility," Bertie said firmly.

"My daughter has no friends who are vulgar enough to think

that spectacle was funny!" Mrs. Blackwater roared, making several of the spectators jump.

"I'm sure she doesn't," Jillian said soothingly as she edged her grandmother back away from the scowling woman. "But Gordon is a young man, and young men often have prankster friends."

Mrs. Blackwater sniffed. "That's true. And having met his family, they do strike me as common. I'm beginning to think this young man is every bit as inappropriate as the last one. Alice is my only child, and I think she should have what's best for her."

Jillian wasn't going to touch any of those remarks with a ten-foot pole. She nodded slightly at Bertie to signal that she'd handle Mrs. Blackwater. Her grandmother gave the taller woman one last glare, then headed into the kitchen. Jillian plastered what she hoped was a sympathetic smile on her face. "Your daughter came in this morning. I returned Chess to her. She seemed very upset about the incident and believes she actually saw Jacob."

"My daughter has a vivid imagination."

"So you don't believe that's possible."

"That she saw a ghost? Hardly."

"I meant, you don't think it's possible that Jacob is alive and could return."

The tall woman lifted one shoulder in a slight shrug. "I suppose he could be alive. No body was ever found. Apparently, he was off on some bizarre jaunt to the Okefenokee Swamp, of all the dismal places. I suppose it wouldn't be the first time someone disappeared completely in the swamp. But if he did return, my daughter still wouldn't marry him. Our family doesn't need that sort of person connected to it."

Curious in spite of herself, Jillian asked, "What sort of person was he?"

Mrs. Blackwater didn't answer immediately, and Jillian tensed, waiting to be told that it was none of her business, which it wasn't.

But instead, the tall woman finally spoke quite civilly. "Jacob Zimmer was a surprisingly studious young man and well-spoken. He was quite different from the boys Alice had dated in high school. One of those actually had the nerve to come to the house to pick up Alice on a motorcycle. You can imagine how quickly I sent him on his way. At the time they were dating, I believed Jacob would be a stabilizing influence on Alice, until I discovered his secret activities."

"Secret activities?" Jillian echoed.

Mrs. Blackwater looked down her nose at Jillian in a cold stare for a moment, then went on as if Jillian hadn't spoken. "Jacob ran a small antique shop at the edge of town, though I never saw anything in there that I would put in my house. When he proposed to Alice, it seemed we would finally see her settled, but then Jacob disappeared in the swamp."

"Did he go out in the swamp often?" Jillian asked.

"Yes, he did. It was one of the few things that he and Alice argued about," Mrs. Blackwater said. "She hated missing so many weekends together because he was on another swamp trip, sometimes with Gordon, sometimes alone."

"What did they do out there?" Jillian asked. "Fishing?"

"His activities would not cast an encouraging light on our family, so I would rather not discuss them," Mrs. Blackwater said. "What does it matter anyway? Young men do silly things when they're far from civilizing influences. Honestly, I would prefer you simply dropped it." She sighed. "I know the prank last night wasn't your fault. It's just so annoying, and I find I have a lack of people to blame."

It would be nice if you picked someone other than us, Jillian thought, but she kept the smile glued to her face. "I understand. I'm sure all the wedding preparations are quite stressful." *I know they are for me.*

Mrs. Blackwater actually smiled. "Yes, they are. You're kind to be so understanding. I will let you return to work. I know you must have plenty to do for the wedding tomorrow."

"I do," Jillian said, then her gaze drifted to the counter area where Maggie was waving at her frantically. "Would you excuse me a moment?"

The tall woman nodded. "I should be on my way. I'll see you tomorrow."

When Jillian reached the counter, Maggie leaned over and spoke in a loud whisper, holding out the phone. "The florist is on the phone and wants to know where you are. She's at Belle Haven with the flowers."

Jillian groaned. "She said early afternoon. And why is she calling the shop instead of my cell phone?"

She brought the phone to her ear in time to hear the woman on the other end say, "Because your cell phone is rolling to voice mail. And I clearly told you last night that I would have the flowers by midmorning."

"You said you could have the rehearsal dinner centerpieces by midmorning," Jillian said. "You said the wedding flowers would arrive in early afternoon."

"I'm sure you're mistaken," the woman said, her voice tight. "But I have them here at Belle Haven, and no one seems to be around to receive them."

Jillian fleetingly wondered where her aunt might be, considering Cornelia had told her she wasn't leaving the house. "I'm leaving the bakery right now. I'll be there as soon as I can." She hurried into the back to grab her purse and give Bertie a quick explanation of why she was rushing off again.

"Fine, fine," her grandmother said. "You should stay at the house and focus on the wedding preparations. I'll see you this evening."

"Thanks, Bertie," Jillian said, giving her grandmother a

quick peck on the cheek, which made the older woman blush and grumble.

Though Jillian normally made it a point to admire the some of the stately old homes that still remained on the drive from the bakery to Belle Haven, her mind was swirling with thoughts of Mrs. Blackwater, her daughter, and the horrible trick played on them.

She pulled her white Prius behind the brightly painted florist's van. As she climbed out of her car, the driver's side and passenger doors of the van flung open, and two women hopped out.

The driver was a woman, around forty, with short blonde hair and broad shoulders. Jillian recognized her immediately as Lilly Quest, the owner of Quest for Beauty. The other woman was at least ten years younger and had the same blonde hair, though it hung from a ponytail. She looked so much like the driver, Jillian thought they were probably sisters.

Lilly frowned at Jillian as she strode toward her. "I've been waiting for nearly an hour."

"I'm sorry to hear that. It is still at least an hour earlier than you said you'd be bringing the flowers," Jillian responded, determined not to be bullied simply because the florist got her times mixed up. After the near catastrophe with the rehearsal dinner centerpieces, she was certainly not going to be pushed around.

The woman gave Jillian a long, silent look, then simply turned and flung open the rear doors on the van. "We should get these inside."

"Excellent idea," Jillian said. She turned a quick smile toward the quieter of the two and offered her hand. "I'm Jillian."

"I'm Rose," the other woman said. "Temporary manual labor for my sister."

Lilly cleared her throat. "It won't take long for the heat to wilt these flowers."

"I hope they can stand at least a little heat since the wedding will be in the garden tomorrow and you promised we'd have heat-hearty arrangements."

"Only plastic flowers are completely wilt proof," Lilly said. Then she thrust a tall vase of flowers into Jillian's arms. "I'll follow you."

"We'll put them in the dining room," Jillian said, backing up quickly before the bossy woman could shove a second heavy arrangement into her arms. "There's plenty of room there, and it's one of the rooms where the air conditioning seems to work best."

The florist handed an arrangement to her sister and grabbed two others. They trooped up to the house, and Jillian shifted the arrangement to one hand so she could open the door. "Right through those French doors," she said. Thankfully, the doors to the dining room were already open, so Jillian didn't have to race the women across the foyer.

Lilly swept by her as if the arrangements she carried were weightless. Her sister followed along, pausing only to roll her eyes at Jillian. Jillian followed them into the dining room and set her arrangement on the long table. "I'll leave you ladies for a moment. I need to check on things out back."

The florist gave her another hard look, clearly less than thrilled that Jillian didn't intended to help carry in the flowers, but she didn't complain. Jillian hurried through the house to the living room and then outside onto the back porch. She spotted Cornelia immediately, standing near the men working on the stage. By the way her great-aunt was waving her hands, it appeared she was directing the work.

With a moan, Jillian hoped Cornelia hadn't insisted the men do anything different from the original plan. She quickly hurried across to her aunt, then nearly stumbled when she recognized one of the workers. It was probably the last man in Moss Hollow that Jillian ever expected to see on his knees with his sleeves rolled up and a hammer in his hand.

"Hunter?" she said.

Hunter Greyson looked up at Jillian and grinned, white teeth dazzling against tan skin. He scrambled to his feet, dusting off the knees of his slacks. "Jillian! I dropped by to ask you a question and saw the guys out here building a stage. I haven't had a chance to swing a hammer in years, so I bullied my way in."

Jillian didn't know what to say to that. She always pictured Hunter in the well-tailored suits he wore as a mortician with his family business, Greyson & Sons Funeral Home, though now that she looked at him more closely, she suspected the dusty slacks he presently wore were part of one of those suits. "It was kind of you to help," she managed.

"It was kind of Harold to let me," Hunter said. He looked around the back garden. "This is going to be a beautiful spot for the wedding reception."

"You know about the wedding?" Jillian asked. She knew she sounded impossibly slow, but the shock was only beginning to wear off.

"Yes," Hunter said, still grinning down at her. "I'm attending. I thought you had the guest list."

"I do," Jillian said, a frown forming between her eyes. "I don't remember your name." *I certainly would have noticed.*

Hunter looked mildly surprised. "Well, I got an invitation. Maybe there were some guests that didn't make it to the list?"

The very thought of her numbers being off for the wedding and the reception made Jillian feel vaguely nauseous. "I'll need to call Mrs. Blackwater," she said faintly.

"I'd imagine." His expression turned concerned. "Are you all right? You look pale suddenly."

Jillian forced a smile. "I'm fine. You had something you wanted to ask me?"

Now it was Hunter's turn to look nervous. "I was just wondering . . . Since you're going to have to be at the wedding and I'm going to be at the wedding, would you be my plus one?"

"Oh, I don't know that I'd be good company," Jillian answered. "I'll be running around the whole time."

"Then I'll chase after you," he said, his smile returning.

Jillian was saved from coming up with a response when a bloodcurdling scream split the air.

6

Jillian raced for the house with Hunter beside her. The scream had to have come from Lilly or Rose as there was no one else inside. They raced through the house, meeting Rose as she thundered in through the front door. She caught sight of Jillian and said, "Lilly?"

They hurried into the dining room, where they found Lilly Quest huddled behind one of the dining room chairs, her back pressed against the wall.

"Lilly?" Rose repeated. "Are you all right?"

"I saw one of those horrible beasts," Lilly whispered as she pressed a shaking hand to her chest. "It came right into the room."

"A beast?" Hunter echoed.

Rose sighed. "A cat. Do y'all have a cat?"

Jillian nodded. "My grandmother does." She looked around the dining room. "I don't see him."

"He was in here," Lilly insisted. "He came right at me, but he ran away when I screamed."

"Possum is harmless," Jillian said. *And you probably scared him half to death.*

"My sister is phobic of cats," Rose said quietly. "If we'd known you had one, she never would have come in the house."

"In that case, perhaps you should wait in the van," Jillian said, turning her attention back to the trembling woman. "I can help Rose carry in the rest of the flowers."

"I'll lend a hand too," Hunter said.

Lilly peered around Jillian. "Are you certain that creature is gone?"

"I can check." Jillian walked around the foyer but saw no sign of

Possum. She assumed the cat had rushed for the safety of upstairs when he heard the screaming. After a last peek behind all the furniture, she stepped back in the dining room. "The coast is clear."

Lilly didn't answer, but she did nod and step out from behind the chair. She allowed her sister to lead her outside, though her gaze darted around the foyer as she hurried through. As soon as she got out the door, she practically ran for the van.

Rose sighed. "She'll be all right now. I'm sorry for the disturbance."

"I'm sorry your sister had such a fright," Jillian said as she followed the younger woman to the van.

With Hunter's help, they quickly unloaded the rest of the flowers. The second the last arrangement was removed, Lilly cranked up the van, the revving motor making it plain she was eager to leave. Rose offered one more apology before hurrying to hop into the van before her sister left without her.

"It must be terrible to be so afraid of something," Hunter said as they watched the van vanish down the driveway. He glanced down at his watch and frowned. "I need to go collect my jacket. I have barely enough time to shower before meeting Savannah."

For a moment, Jillian was surprised, but then she remembered her friend handled the bookkeeping for Greyson & Sons, as well as for most of the other businesses in Moss Hollow. Bertie even let Savannah help out The Chocolate Shoppe at tax time, which was a big concession for her grandmother, who could be a control enthusiast.

"Thank you so much for helping out with the stage," Jillian said.

"My pleasure," he said, giving her another look at his dazzling smile. It really was no wonder he was considered the most eligible bachelor in Moss Hollow, at least by the older women in the Sweetie Pies, who constantly encouraged her to snap him up while she could, as if he were some kind of fish she needed to catch. "But you never told me if you'd be my date."

"Oh, right." Jillian felt her cheeks warm. "If you don't mind how busy I'll be, then yes."

After Hunter left, Jillian checked in with the stage building and found the men were nearly finished. Cornelia had lost interest in supervising and was wandering in the back garden. Jillian walked back to join her great-aunt.

Cornelia looked at her sharply. "What was that shrieking about? I thought perhaps it was the haint, but she never appears so early in the day."

Or at all, Jillian thought. "Actually Possum was terrorizing the florist."

"Pishposh, Raymond would never frighten someone. He's a dear."

"I hope you're feeling better back here today," Jillian said.

"The specter has gone," Cornelia said. "After last night, it's clear he's connected with the wedding party, not with us."

"I agree with that, though I don't think he's an actual specter. Still, I wish I knew why someone would play such a cruel trick on our clients."

Cornelia gazed distractedly off into the woods. "Perhaps they paid a cruel trick on him first." She turned to look at Jillian. "Maybe you should find out more about what happened to the poor man."

"Alice Blackwater said something very similar earlier today."

Cornelia smiled. "Then it's probably fate."

Jillian barely suppressed the urge to roll her eyes at her aunt. "Well, don't overdo it out here. I need to go inside and obsess over my lists."

She found her clipboard on the breakfast table where she'd left it. She poured herself a glass of sweet tea and settled down at the table, which reminded her that she needed to call Mrs. Blackwater about the guest list. Unfortunately, the woman's phone rolled immediately to voice mail. Jillian left a message, then turned back to flipping through the pages on her clipboard, her mind turning again and again to the question of who had played the awful prank at the rehearsal dinner and why.

Finally, Jillian dropped the clipboard on the table, deciding she would have to feed her curiosity before she could concentrate on her real work.

She walked to her home office, off the foyer. Their redecorating budget hadn't extended to that room either, so the walls were covered in old, striped wallpaper, slightly faded from the light coming in the two tall windows. A brick fireplace at the opposite end of the room had a beautiful carved mantel that had once been white to match the deep crown molding at the top of the walls. An old, slightly faded Persian rug covered the floor. A vintage horsehair sofa, which had been moved from the living room when they redecorated that space, faced the fireplace. An old rolltop desk against the wall opposite the windows held Jillian's laptop. She'd finally resolved Bertie's issues with the cable company and no longer had to rely on dial-up Internet access, for which she was truly grateful. Altogether, the room more resembled a storage area for mismatched furniture than an office, but at least her bedroom didn't double as her office anymore.

Jillian settled into a small vanity chair that didn't match the desk or anything else in the room. Finding a series of online newspaper reports on the disappearance of Jacob Zimmer didn't take long. The first reports were short and full of optimism that the young man would soon be found. Within days, the outlook was considerably less sunny, and statistics about the number of unsolved disappearances in the Okefenokee crept into the narrative.

The one thing that none of the reports included was an explanation of the reason the young man went to the swamp. Jacob was described as familiar with the area and as a frequent visitor to Duvall Island in the Okefenokee National Wildlife Refuge. But none of the accounts mentioned why. Jillian had expected to learn he was an avid fisherman or a hunter, or even a bird-watcher. Though the accounts mentioned his antiques business and his engagement to Alice Blackwater, the only details about his trips to the swamp were that they were frequent, especially to Duvall Island, and that he'd never returned after his last visit.

Despite growing up in Georgia, Jillian had never been to the Okefenokee Swamp. The word *swamp* brought to mind the drone of mosquitos and a fear of lurking alligators. She clicked over to the U.S. Fish & Wildlife Service website for the swamp, looking for more information on reasons people went there. She shuddered as an alligator took up most of the screen on the front page of the site.

"Very inviting," she muttered. To her surprise, she discovered there was more to the swamp than creepy-crawlies. The Okefenokee National Wildlife Refuge even had historical sites, and Duvall Island was one of them. Apparently, it was the homestead of a "swamper" family in the late 1800s.

"What were you looking for out there, Jacob?" Jillian whispered as she looked at photos of the weathered wooden buildings that made up the homestead. She read through blog posts from people who had visited the area, looking for any reason that might repeatedly bring someone to Duvall Island.

Jillian was so engrossed with her reading that when the door to the office creaked open, she spun sharply in her chair and gasped. Her aunt stood in the doorway, her arms full of cat. "Jillian, I've been calling you from the kitchen."

"I'm sorry, Aunt Cornelia," Jillian said, pressing her hand to her chest and feeling her heart pound against her palm. "I got caught up in reading."

Cornelia glanced toward the computer and sniffed. Reading was something one did with books, in Cornelia's opinion, not with a screen. It was an opinion Jillian had heard more than once before, so she was glad when Cornelia limited her censure to a pointed look.

"I was wondering if you'd like some leftover soup from last night," Cornelia said. "I was going to warm some up for myself, and I thought I might go ahead and put the whole pot on the stove. I know Bertie will be hungry when she gets home."

"That sounds good," Jillian said as she shut down her computer. "Did the guys finish the stage?"

"Heavens, yes," Cornelia said. "It looks nice. Do you want to set up furniture for the wedding and the reception tonight?"

Jillian shook her head. "No, then we'd have to wipe everything down when the dew falls. I don't want to risk anyone sitting on something wiggly from the woods. Savannah and Laura Lee are coming early to help set up, along with Lenora's cousin, Virgil."

"Well, speak of the devil," Cornelia said, pointing through the window toward the front driveway. "Isn't that Savannah's car?"

Jillian stood and looked out the window. "It sure is." When her friend hopped out of the car, Jillian waved. She walked through the foyer and outside. "Hi! You didn't get confused about when we're supposed to set up for the wedding, did you?"

Savannah shook her head. "I came out to whisk you away. With everything you have to do tomorrow, you need some time to kick back and relax, so I'm taking you out to dinner."

Jillian shifted nervously. "I don't know. I should go over my lists again."

"If I know you, Jillian Green, and I do, you've looked over those lists a zillion times. But if it'll get you out of the house, you can go get them, and we can look over them together while we eat."

Jillian cast a last glance toward the house, then shook her

head. "No, you're right. I've been over and over them. It will be nice to go do something fun. I need to let Cornelia know since she was about to heat up some soup."

"We'll invite her to come along, if she wants."

Cornelia declared Savannah to be "just darling" for asking, but she wasn't interested in going out to dinner. "There's nothing at the restaurant that will taste any better than Bertie's soup," she said. "Besides, I want to have it all warmed up when my sister gets home. She's as bad as Jillian for not taking proper care of herself."

"Do you think we should wait and take Bertie out?" Savannah asked.

Both Cornelia and Jillian laughed at that. "Bertie doesn't believe in restaurants," Jillian said. "Paying money for someone else to cook a dinner that isn't nearly as good as her own doesn't make sense to her. My grandmother can be frugal."

"Bertie's cheap," Cornelia said. "There's no point beating around the bush about it. But you two go on and have a nice time."

As they drove through the Moss Hollow streets, Savannah asked, "Is Crazy Fish all right?"

Jillian nodded. They'd eaten at the bar and grill before, and the fish was delicious.

The hostess greeted them by name, offering a big smile as she led them to a small table not far from the bar. Jillian almost asked for a different table, but it was probably early enough that it wouldn't be particularly loud.

Jillian was always charmed by the colorful wooden fish on the walls, but she quickly turned to the menu. As she looked over the offerings, her stomach growled, reminding her that she'd skipped lunch. Again. She'd done far too much of that since taking on the wedding planning.

At another, louder growl from Jillian's stomach, Savannah giggled. "Apparently, I'm feeding you just in time."

Jillian pressed a hand to her stomach. "Sorry about that. I'm really trying to stop skipping meals. I get busy, and the time rushes by."

"I'm not one to judge," Savannah said. "During tax season, I'm lucky to catch lunch a couple times a week." She looked at Jillian over her menu. "Hunter said you had some excitement at the house."

For a moment, Jillian had no idea what she meant, then the memory of the terrified florist came back. "Oh, yes, the poor florist with the cat phobia."

"Bless her heart," Savannah said. "That must be awful. I can't think of anything that scares me that much. Maybe snakes."

Jillian shivered at the thought. "Thankfully, we're not likely to run into any snakes at the mansion. Not inside anyway. I'm also hoping we don't run into anymore uninvited ghosts."

"That was one weird practical joke," Savannah agreed. "Who could possibly find that funny?"

"You talking about Jacob's ghost?"

The women turned to see a young man perched on one of the barstools and looking their way. "Sorry to interrupt. I was at the rehearsal dinner last night. I don't know if you remember me."

Jillian hated to admit that the man didn't look particularly familiar and was relieved when Savannah jumped in. "Of course I remember you," she said. "You don't like iced tea. I thought it was brave of you to admit that, considering we're deep in the heart of Dixie."

The young man grinned. "The only iced tea I drink has the words 'Long Island' in front of the name, but the food was great last night. On the other hand, the floor show was plain creepy."

"It wasn't my doing," Jillian said. "I don't know who thought that would be a good practical joke on the bride and groom."

"Yeah, it definitely wasn't cool. I don't know Gordon all that well, but I can't see anyone doing that to Alice. She's spoiled, but she's not a horrible person."

Jillian was prevented from asking more questions when the waitress showed up to rattle off the nightly specials and take their drink orders. They both ordered sweet tea, and the young man at the bar chuckled at their choice. As soon as the waitress walked away, Jillian turned her attention back to the stranger. "You're a groomsman, but you don't know the groom?"

"Alice is my cousin," he said, then he slid off the stool and walked over to offer his hand. "I'm Louis Blackwater. The mayor's my uncle."

Jillian shook the young man's hand. "How good a look did you get at the so-called ghost?" Jillian asked after Louis and Savannah exchanged introductions. "Did it look like Jacob Zimmer?"

Louis shrugged and shoved his hands in his jeans pockets. "I was distracted by Alice's fainting spell. Plus, the creepy dude had mud all over his face. It could have been my brother and I might not have recognized him."

"But Alice seemed to," Jillian said.

"She's always been prone to imagining weird stuff, so I'm not surprised she immediately assumed it was Jacob. We all did. Plus, I think she never really got over Jacob's disappearance."

"What was Jacob doing in the swamp?" Jillian asked. "I understand he went there often. Was he a fisherman or a hunter or something?"

"I don't know," Louis said. "He never offered me any fish or venison, but I didn't really know Jacob that well either. He was standoffish with the family and behaved as if everything was some big secret. Plus, he ran an antique store, so clearly he and I had *nothing* in common. I suspect my uncle knew more about him. Uncle Carl is easier to deal with than my aunt." He smiled. "You've probably noticed that."

"A little," Jillian agreed, not wanting to be caught complaining. "I understand Jacob was Gordon's best friend."

"I guess." He shrugged again. "I don't really hang with Alice that much now that we're all grown up. I mean, I've seen Gordon a couple times at family things. He's friendly enough." His grin turned sly. "You'd better not let Aunt Mary know you're gossiping about the family. She'll have you flogged, or at least you'll feel like you were."

"Alice asked me to help her figure out what's going on," Jillian said. "Otherwise, I'm not interested in gossip."

The young man rocked on his heels and looked at Jillian with interest. "So you're a detective too? That's full-service event planning."

"Considering that Jacob—or the specter or whoever it was— definitely ruined the rehearsal dinner for my client, I want to know who is behind the prank for my own sake," Jillian said.

Louis raised his eyebrows. "That's a thought. Maybe someone pulled that stunt to ruin the rehearsal dinner. You know anyone who wants to throw a wrench into your business?"

Jillian blinked in surprise at the question. She hadn't even considered that. What if the specter was less about Alice and more about ruining Jillian's business?

She shook her head. That was ridiculous. Who could possibly want to see her fail? "That's pretty far-fetched."

"I do love discussing conspiracy theories with ladies in bars—"

"Technically," Savannah interrupted, "we're in the restaurant area."

He nodded concession. "Good point. Make that discussing conspiracy theories with ladies in restaurants. But I need to head on home. I reckon I'll see you both tomorrow at the wedding?"

"I'm sure," Jillian said. "Thanks for your insight on the prank."

"Don't know how insightful I was. Y'all have a good evening."

As the door swung shut behind Louis, the server arrived with their iced teas. Jillian drummed her fingers on the table impatiently, eager for the server to take their orders and leave. Savannah looked pointedly at Jillian's fingers, and Jillian dropped her hands into her lap. She ordered the fish and chips, giving the waitress a pleasant smile to make up for her impatience.

As soon as the waitress finished and hurried off to the kitchen, Jillian turned to Savannah. "Do *you* think the specter could be someone targeting me and my business?"

"That would be rather extreme," Savannah answered. "I can only think of one person I've even heard complain about the expansion."

"You've heard someone complain about my event planning?" Jillian asked. "And you didn't tell me?"

"I'm a bookkeeper," Savannah answered. "I hear a lot of people complain about a lot of businesses."

Jillian leaned on her forearms. "Who? Who complained?"

"Richard Meyer at Dreams Come True," Savannah said. "Since he used The Chocolate Shoppe to cater a couple of his wine-and-chocolate events, he feels it's disloyal of y'all to expand into his territory."

"Good heavens, we've fallen into an Old West movie," Jillian said. "Surely there's enough business for both of us."

Savannah nodded and took a long sip of her tea. "I'm sure there is. It was only a passing remark."

"What does Richard Meyer look like?" Jillian asked.

"Medium height, slight build," Savannah said.

Jillian pressed her lips together. "That's interesting. Now I wonder what he looks like dripping with mud and moss."

"That I couldn't tell you. He's fairly moss-free when I meet with him to go over his books."

Jillian idly stirred the ice cubes around in her glass with a straw. Maybe she'd been looking at the specter all wrong. Could Dreams Come True be trying to turn her new business into a nightmare? And if so, were they done trying?

Saturday morning proved to have absolutely perfect weather. The sky was clear, but a breeze kept the sun from being stifling. Jillian rose well before dawn to run around wildly, finishing up all the last-minute preparations.

When the bride and her attendants arrived, Alice scurried up to the room Jillian had designated as a changing area on the second floor, along with her giggling attendants. Jillian was glad to hear no more talk about the rehearsal dinner visitor. She walked outside to check on the garden area where Lenora's cousin, Virgil, was helping Harold Johnson set up the canopies she'd ordered to help shade the wedding guests from the sun.

She was pleased to see they were nearly done. Harold caught sight of her and waved. "We'll be out of your way in about five minutes."

"No hurry," Jillian said. "I'm doing my impression of a chicken with its head cut off."

The older man looked around. "Well, everything looks good. Thank you for thinking of me when you needed help."

Jillian smiled. The odd jobs he'd done to help her get ready for the wedding were a far cry from his normal work as a groundskeeper. She was lucky he didn't consider the work beneath him, since he certainly did a great job. "I'm grateful for your help."

"And mine?" Virgil asked as he dusted off his hands.

"Yes, of course," Jillian said. "And yours. You've both saved me. I'd been away from Moss Hollow for a lot of years, so I'm lucky to have skilled people to call on when I need help."

Lenora's cousin puffed out his chest. "You can call on me anytime." He gave her a sly smile and a wink. "Leastways, anytime you can pay."

"I wouldn't think of asking you to work for nothing," Jillian said. Lenora had once told her that Virgil didn't do anything for free, and she certainly believed it.

She noticed that the temperature under the canopy was markedly cooler. At least she wouldn't have to worry about guests passing out from the heat. She checked on all the flowers and was relieved to see that none of them looked wilted. Now if they'd only stay perky through the service.

A finger poked her in the back, making her jump. She spun to face a teenager in one of the pale-blue, strapless bridesmaid's dresses. A small top hat in matching blue perched at a saucy angle on the girl's limp brown hair. Although the slightly built girl didn't quite fill out the front of the dress, the color certainly complemented her pale skin, though the bored look on her face did not. "Alice wants to talk to you."

"Does she need help?" Jillian asked. "Is something wrong?"

The girl shook her head and shrugged. "She said she wanted to talk to you."

"Tell her I'll be right there."

"Okay." The girl spun and dashed for the house, holding up the wads of chiffon in her skirt as she ran.

Jillian held her breath, hoping the girl didn't trip and fall. She had no way to clean or mend the dress in time if she did. Thankfully, the girl made it through the front door.

After a quick check on how things were going in the kitchen with the food for the reception, Jillian trotted upstairs to check on the bride. The changing room was one of the unused upstairs bedrooms. With most of the furniture carted off to the attic, the room now sported a slightly mismatched collection of cozy seating, a clothing rack, one three-way mirror, several full-length mirrors, and two long tables for guests to lay out makeup and to hold a supply of bottled water. Though the clothing rack was well supplied with hangers, the bridal party had draped clothes over the rack and across several pieces of furniture. Chess lay on a blazer, left discarded on a floral love seat. The cat was looking down with annoyance at a little girl who wore a perfect replica of the classic Alice dress, with the long blond hair to match. The little girl was alternately petting the cat's tail and giving it small tugs.

Alice stood in front of the three-way mirror, smoothing the front of her gown nervously. The dress had a heavily embroidered corset top that laced up in the back. The white-on-white embroidery of the corset featured roses, watches, and teacups. Since her mother had vetoed Alice's desire to wear the classic blue-and-white *Alice in Wonderland* style, she'd gone with a custom-made gown that probably cost as much as all the other wedding preparations combined.

Alice turned worried eyes toward Jillian. "Have you seen Gordon?"

"No, but he said he only needed a changing room for after the ceremony," she said. "I believe he was planning to arrive in his tux, so there's still plenty of time."

Alice nodded. "I know, but I called him last night and he didn't answer."

"He was probably out with the guys," said one of the other bridesmaids, a woman about Alice's age with a head of black curls who was carefully pinning a small, pale-blue top hat in place on her head. "You're such a worrywart, Alice."

"It's not like him not to call me back."

Alice reached up to nibble at the corner of one of her fingernails and a different bridesmaid slapped her hand away. "Don't you dare ruin that manicure! Honestly, Gordon will be here soon, and you'll get married. It's all going to be fine."

"I'm sure everything *will* be fine," Jillian said gently. "But I'll check downstairs for Gordon and send word the second he arrives."

Alice managed a weak smile. "Thank you."

Jillian left the room and hurried down to the foyer where several of the groomsmen were wiling away time inside with the air conditioning. On the foyer tables, beside flower arrangements that matched the ones outside, Jillian had bottled water tucked into small buckets filled with ice. Until time for the wedding, the wedding party that didn't need a changing area could use the foyer and the living room to stay out of the heat. At Mrs. Blackwater's request, Jillian limited refreshments to water to avoid clothing mishaps.

Spotting Louis Blackwater, Jillian turned in his direction. In the pale-blue tuxedo, the young man looked positively elegant. He saw Jillian coming his way and smiled. "Everything looks really great."

"Thank you," Jillian said, casting a quick look around the foyer and noting a couple of empty water bottles she'd need to grab when she left the room. "Have you seen Gordon?"

Louis shook his head. "Nope, no sign of the groom yet, though all the rest of us are here."

"I'm sure he'll be here any minute," Jillian said, forcing false confidence into her tone. "Your cousin is a little worried."

"She's like that. I'll keep an eye out, and when I see him, I'll let Alice know."

Jillian smiled. "Thank you. Are your aunt and uncle here yet?"

Louis shook his head. "I have seen a couple of folks arrive in the last few minutes, though, and head for the chairs." He nodded toward the front windows that looked out toward the garden area where the wedding canopy shaded a small handful of guests.

Jillian noted with relief that the ushers were already on duty, leading people to the proper seats. A young girl, a few years older than the one upstairs but wearing another perfect replica of the *Alice* gown, stood next to a white stand at the back of the chairs, encouraging everyone to sign the guest book. Everything looked picture perfect.

Her feeling of confidence was short-lived when a striking gray Mercedes pulled up and let Mary Blackwater off at the front door before pulling away to park. The mother of the bride didn't even glance in the direction of the guest seating and instead marched up the stairs to the house with a purposeful stride and a look of doom.

Jillian opened the front door for her client and received a scowl in response. "My daughter has been texting me every five minutes. I understand her fiancé has vanished?"

"He hasn't arrived yet," Jillian said. "And he's not answering his phone. Beyond that, I think it's a little early to say he's vanished."

Mrs. Blackwater's expression darkened still more. "He'd best not stand up my daughter at the altar!"

"I'm sure it's a little premature to jump to that conclusion," Jillian said.

"Aunt Mary, chill!" Louis said, appearing suddenly at Jillian's elbow. "You know how easily Alice freaks out. Considering what happened to Jacob, I think you ought to be impressed she's not running through the house shrieking."

"I am dazzled by her restraint," Mrs. Blackwater said dryly.

Louis shrugged. "I'm sure Gordon will be here soon." He raised his eyebrows slightly. "Hey, I know a guy who lives in Gordon's apartment complex. I can send him over to knock on the door. Maybe Gordon got trashed last night and slept through his alarm."

"That would be inexcusable behavior on his part!" Mrs. Blackwater said darkly.

Louis shrugged, then grinned at his aunt. It was clear he wasn't the least bit intimidated by her. "If I were getting married today, you can bet I would have done a lot of drinking last night."

"That's because you take after your father," Mrs. Blackwater muttered. "Have your friend check on Gordon."

Pulling his phone from his rear pocket, Louis nodded at his aunt. "Sure thing. Give me a second." He backed away while he made the call.

Mrs. Blackwater turned her full attention to Jillian. "Go and tell my daughter that we are here and that we're handling the situation with Gordon."

Jillian felt a momentary flash of annoyance at being ordered around, but then realized she should be grateful for the excuse to get away from the overbearing woman, so she nodded and practically ran for the stairs.

She was within three steps of the second-floor landing when she spotted Possum, sitting on the floor right outside the door to the changing room. The cat was staring pointedly at the crack under the door and lashing his tail. "Who let you out of Aunt Cornelia's room?" Jillian asked.

At virtually the same moment, she heard a voice call behind her. "Jillian!"

Jillian stopped at the top of the stairs and turned to see Hunter Greyson striding along the balcony toward her. "I've been looking for you."

Alice, who was in the changing room, must have heard the voices from the balcony, because she chose that moment to fling open the door. This offered Chess an opportunity to escape the bored attention of the little flower girl. The cat rocketed past his mistress and out the door. Possum raced after Chess, both heading right for the stairs.

Jillian stepped down to give herself a better chance to catch one or both cats before they could race down the stairs. It was a good plan, but she didn't take Hunter into account. He had reached the top of the stairs when both cats connected with him right at the edge of the top step. Just as the tall mortician was taking a step, Chess shoved her way between Hunter's legs, followed by Possum who slammed into him.

What followed seemed to Jillian to be a kind of slow-motion horror, and she was unable to stop it. Hunter stumbled and fell from the top step, colliding hard with Jillian. Hunter's momentum and weight meant Jillian stood no chance of stopping his fall. The two of them tangled together, rolling halfway down the flight of stairs.

Stars burst into Jillian's field of vision as her head slammed into either the wall or one of the steps. She wasn't sure which it was, knowing only that it hurt. She heard fabric rip and had a brief moment to hope that when they landed, she wouldn't find unfortunate body parts revealed.

When they stopped tumbling, Jillian took a shaky breath and assessed her condition. Her head hurt a lot, and the rest of her body was registering complaints as well. She suspected she was going to have some spectacular bruises.

"Jillian," Hunter said, and Jillian saw he was cradling one forearm in the other. "Are you all right?"

"I'm fine," she said. "How about you?"

"I think I may have broken my arm." He looked at her apologetically. "I'm so sorry if I have spoiled your event."

"Don't worry about it," Jillian said. "I'll call an ambulance and get you to the hospital." She shifted to reach the phone in her blazer pocket, and her head protested painfully. "Ouch." She lifted a hand to touch the sore spot, then gasped when it came away wet. Looking down at her bloody fingers, Jillian suddenly didn't feel well at all. She felt woozy and sick to her stomach.

"You're bleeding!" Hunter said, his voice full of alarm.

I noticed, she thought. She wondered how quickly she could get the bleeding stopped. More guests were beginning to arrive. She didn't have time to bleed. Forgetting her earlier plan to call an ambulance, Jillian struggled to stand.

"You should probably stay seated," Hunter suggested, reaching for her with his uninjured arm.

Jillian decided he was right when she made it to her feet and the room spun. She wobbled, grabbing one of the stair railings with a blood-smeared hand. Her fingers slipped on the glossy wood railing, leaving behind a red streak. *I need to get that off there before Bertie sees it*, she thought.

"Jillian, sit down at once!"

Jillian started at the sound of her grandmother's voice. It was as if her thought about the older woman had made her appear. "I can't," Jillian insisted. "I have a wedding to handle."

"We'll take care of it."

Jillian blinked at the gentle sound of her friend Savannah's voice. *When did Savannah get here? Oh, right, she came early. Why is she on the stairs, though?* Jillian finally gave in to the pounding headache and the insistence of her family and friends that she stop resisting and let them handle things. Gentle hands supported her as she was half carried to the dining room to wait on the ambulance. Hunter sat in a chair beside her, still cradling his arm.

"I'm sorry I hurt you," he said.

Jillian shook her head, then moaned as she realized head shaking was a bad idea. "It was Possum and Chess. I'm sorry you're hurt." She managed a weak smile. "Will you let me sign your cast?"

"I don't know if doctors still do casts these days," he said, his smile considerably warmer. "But if they do, you can be the first to sign it."

When the ambulance arrived, the paramedics poked at her head and made her headache worse before they packed them up to head to the hospital. Jillian caught sight of a disapproving glare from Mrs. Blackwater as they were wheeled out of the house.

So much for my event-planning business, she thought. *I'll be lucky if we're allowed to plan a kid's birthday party after this fiasco.*

8

Since neither Jillian nor Hunter had life-threatening injuries, they found they weren't exactly priority patients in the emergency room. More than an hour passed before either of them even saw a doctor. On the upside, Hunter's arm wasn't fractured, though Jillian knew the wrenching sprain Hunter had suffered was probably as painful as many breaks and could be nearly as slow to heal.

For Jillian, the most horrific part of the experience was having a small circle of hair shaved on the side of her head to accommodate the stitches for the gash. It would take some creative hairstyling to hide that.

"Your pupils are equal and reactive," the doctor said after flashing a painfully bright light past her eyes so many times she was considering snatching it away from him and smacking him with it. The doctor was a short man with a craggy face and a fluff of white hair that reminded Jillian of Albert Einstein. "But you seem to have some light sensitivity."

"A little," Jillian admitted, wincing as he flashed the light again, making her suspect the man was sadistic.

"Any nausea?" he asked.

"No," she lied, but then thought better of it. "Maybe a little."

"You may have a slight concussion," he said. "Certainly you will need to take things easy for the next few days, and you'll want to see your primary-care physician in about a week or so to have the stitches removed."

She winced at the thought. "Will I be able to go soon?"

"Let's wait a while longer, to be sure," he said. "Then you'll be cleared to go home as long as you have someone with you. Do you live alone?"

"No, I live with my grandmother and great-aunt at Belle Haven."

The doctor raised matching white caterpillar eyebrows. "Belle Haven? Cornelia and Bertie?"

"Yes, Bertie Harper is my grandmother."

The doctor's face split in a grin, showing off small, slightly crooked teeth. "I went to school with those two. Prettiest girls in Moss Hollow with those blue eyes and blonde curls. I had such a crush on Bertie."

That shocking revelation seemed to fit right into the day Jillian was having. "Isn't it a small world?" she said.

"Definitely." The man was still muttering about Bertie's blue eyes as he wandered out of the cubicle.

Jillian looked across the room to where Hunter sat on a matching exam table with his arm in a sling.

"Are you still in pain?" he asked.

Jillian remembered not to nod. "A little," she said. "And you?"

"I'm feeling amazing." He managed a small smile. "That's the positive side of having a sprain over a head injury. I get pain medication."

"I'm so sorry for all of this, Hunter," she said.

"I certainly don't hold you responsible," he insisted. "Especially since you aren't blaming me for falling on you. You could have been seriously injured."

"Thankfully, we'll both be fine." Jillian looked down at her watch and groaned. "The bride and groom should be saying their vows right about now. I hope I can get back in time to help out with the reception."

"I'm certain the doctors want you take it easy for a while," Hunter said. "I heard that you might have a mild concussion. Running a wedding reception is not going to help you recover."

"I won't run it," Jillian said. "I'll only watch over it. That's assuming someone lets me out of here before the reception is over."

As it turned out, neither Jillian nor Hunter had to wait much longer. The doctor gave Jillian a list of things she shouldn't do and what she could take for the headache. "Mostly you need to rest. You should be back to normal in a few days."

There's that word again, Jillian thought. *Days!* Even assuming she didn't help out with the reception, she had piles of work getting Belle Haven back to normal, and there was her usual work at the bakery as well. Jillian couldn't imagine playing the invalid for days.

She discovered that Cornelia had volunteered to drive over and await their discharge. When a volunteer wheeled Jillian out, she spotted her great-aunt listening attentively to a chubby young woman with long black hair, her clothes resembling a trick-or-treat fortune-teller costume. "Where does Cornelia find these people?" Jillian muttered.

"Excuse me?" the volunteer asked.

"Nothing," Jillian said. "I was talking to myself. There's my great-aunt."

Cornelia caught sight of Jillian and hurried over, looking from Jillian to Hunter, who sat in a matching wheelchair with his arm in a sling, pushed by a nearly matching volunteer. "Are you both all right?"

"We'll be fine," Jillian said. "Do you think you can give Hunter a lift also? It's the least we can do, since Possum knocked him down the stairs."

Aunt Cornelia's eyes widened. "I'm certain it was a misunderstanding."

"I don't know how someone can misunderstand having a cat plow into the back of their legs," Jillian said dryly.

"I believe Possum was in pursuit of another cat," Hunter said.

"He wasn't intentionally attacking me."

"Certainly not!" Cornelia huffed. "Raymond doesn't have a violent bone in his body."

"Raymond?" Hunter echoed.

"My late husband," Cornelia said.

Hunter turned a bewildered look toward Jillian, and she refrained from shaking her head. "It's better if you don't think about it, really." She reached up to rub at her temple. "Can we go?"

"Of course. I'll pull the car around." Cornelia looked from Jillian to Hunter and frowned slightly. "I should warn you, it's going to be tight. I didn't think about driving Hunter back so I brought my car."

Aunt Cornelia drove a meticulously restored powder-blue Mustang that had been her husband's pride and joy. She always said she couldn't stand the thought of giving up something Raymond had loved so much. And, besides, she looked good in the car. It matched her eyes.

"I'll ride in the back," Jillian said. "I probably fold up better than Hunter."

"I don't want to put you out," Hunter said. "I could call my assistant, Oliver, and have him come pick me up. He'll need to collect me from the mansion anyway, as I'm not supposed to drive after taking the pain medication."

"Nonsense," Cornelia said. "We'll tuck everyone in my car and figure out how to get you home from the mansion when we get there. Nearly everyone in the Sweetie Pies is helping out at the reception, so we should certainly have enough drivers available to get you and your car home." She bustled off to retrieve the car, and the volunteers wheeled both chairs after her.

As they waited inside the foyer of the emergency room, Jillian noticed Hunter watching her as she rubbed her head and she forced a smile. "I'm fine. When I get back to the house, I'll take something for my headache." *And find out how things are going with the wedding.*

Though Jillian had never been troubled by motion sickness before and despite the smooth ride, the drive back to the mansion left her feeling mildly sick. Jillian assumed it was a combination of her mild concussion, splitting headache and the cramped confines of the tiny backseat. She was glad when the driveway to Belle Haven came into view. As they pulled up the drive, Jillian was shocked to see very few cars. "How could the reception be over already?" she asked.

"I have no idea," Cornelia said as she maneuvered around the cars.

Jillian gritted her teeth as she waited for Hunter to struggle out of the car with his arm in the sling, reminding herself that it wasn't his fault that he didn't have the use of both arms. She squeezed out of the car, discovering that even that movement made the throbbing in her head worse. As soon as she found out what was going on with the reception, she had to get something for her headache.

The front foyer was filled with people, standing around with glasses of lemonade and fussing over Alice Blackwater, who sat in one of two dainty French armchairs that Jillian had moved to the foyer. Alice still wore her wedding gown and sobbed quietly into a snow-white handkerchief. Jillian noticed the other bridesmaids were dressed in casual clothes, as were several of the groomsmen.

"It's about time you got back!" Mrs. Blackwater bellowed at

a volume that cut through Jillian's head like an ax, nearly making her whimper.

"Mary, don't pick on the girl," Mr. Blackwater insisted, laying a hand on his wife's arm. "After all, she was injured by *our* daughter's insane cat."

Mrs. Blackwater sniffed but didn't argue.

Jillian looked around the room, bewildered. "What happened?"

"Gordon was a no-show." Jillian turned to see Louis Blackwater in jeans and a white dress shirt. "When my friend got to his apartment, he found the door ajar and no groom inside."

"Something terrible has happened to him," Alice wailed. "I just know it has."

"He left his apartment door open?" Jillian said. She felt faintly lost, as if her brain was still foggy. The doctor had warned that might be a side effect of the concussion, but Jillian wasn't sure she'd be able to sort it out any better without a conk on the head. "He must have been planning to come right back."

"My friend waited at the apartment for an hour, but Gordon didn't come back in all that time, so he locked up and left," Louis said with a shrug. "At least Gordon should still have all his stuff when he gets home." He dropped his voice as he stepped closer to Jillian. "My aunt told everyone to go on home about thirty minutes ago, but we can't get Alice to leave. She insists Gordon will get here eventually."

"He will!" Alice shrieked at her cousin. "If he can, he will. Gordon did not abandon me."

"Alice, get a grip on yourself," her mother demanded. "Clearly Gordon isn't coming. We need to go home."

Alice flapped a hand at her mother. "You go. All of you go! I'm staying here."

Staring at the distraught young woman, Jillian wasn't aware of what an experienced planner would do in a situation where the bride decided to camp out indefinitely. She certainly didn't want to throw the poor woman out, but she wasn't sure what the bounds of hospitality demanded.

Apparently Aunt Cornelia did. She walked over to pat Alice on the shoulder. "You stay as long as you want. No one is going to make you leave before you're ready." She looked around at the other members of the wedding party. "All of you are welcome to stay."

"We have plenty of food," Bertie spoke from the far end of the foyer. "And I've laid out a small buffet for anyone who would care to eat before you go. I've opened the dining room, which should certainly have enough room for all of you, though you're also welcome to eat in the breakfast room."

Jillian blinked away grateful tears at her grandmother and aunt. She was suddenly very glad she didn't have to figure out what to do next. All she wanted was a tall glass of iced tea and something for her headache. She startled slightly—sending a lancing pain through her head—when Cornelia put a hand on her arm. "Come on to the breakfast room, Jillian, and sit down. You're pale as a ghost."

For once, Jillian didn't argue and let her aunt tow her to the back of the house. Once she was seated at the breakfast table with a glass of sweet tea, she sipped quietly and let the mind fog flow over her. Her first event was in shambles. Surely no one would ever want to use her service again. She could only hope the catastrophe wouldn't taint the bakery.

To Jillian's surprise, about the time she had fallen as deeply as possible into gloom, someone slipped into the chair across from her. She looked up from where she'd been staring at the slowly melting ice cubes in her glass and found herself looking into the swollen eyes of her client. At least Alice had stopped crying.

"I'm sorry that Chess made you fall," Alice said softly. "We still haven't found her." Jillian saw the young woman's eyes glisten, but then Alice blinked rapidly, clearly not wanting to sink back into weeping. "I wanted to ask you something."

"What's that?"

"I want you to find Gordon," she said. "I know you told me you're not a detective and all that, but if you can find him, I'll marry him. Wouldn't that be better for your business? Then your first event would be a success."

"I think you should file a missing person's report," Jillian said quietly. "This is really more a matter for real investigators, the trained kind."

Alice gave her an annoyed frown. "Do you really think anyone will take my report seriously? Half of my wedding party thinks he ran off to avoid having my mom for a mother-in-law."

Jillian hadn't considered that possibility, but it didn't seem that unreasonable. "Well . . ."

"He didn't. He wouldn't. He could be hurt or in danger, and I need to know someone is looking for him. If you'll agree to try, I promise to talk my mother out of refusing to pay you for the work you did."

Jillian snapped to attention at that, and her headache swelled until she nearly whimpered. "Your mother isn't planning to pay me? But I did the work."

Alice shrugged. "My mother isn't known for her rational behavior. Daddy will try to talk her out of it, of course. He's a good guy, but it's going to take both of us. So if you won't agree to look for my benefit, then you might want to do it for yours."

Jillian moaned and gently rubbed at her temple. "What if I *can't* find him?"

"Try," Alice said, clasping her hands together on the table in front of her. "Say you'll try, and I promise you'll get paid. I think you're the kind of person who'll do what she promises, so just promise."

"You aren't giving me much choice."

"That's the idea."

Jillian sighed, lowered her head onto her forearms on the table, and shut her eyes. "Fine. I promise I will try to find Gordon."

Alice gave a squeal of delight and patted Jillian's shoulder. "Thank you. Thank you. I know you'll find him. Everyone says you're stubborn and nosy. That's exactly what I need."

Jillian almost raised her head to rebut the comment about her being nosy, but it seemed too much like work. She had a moment of wondering if Hunter had gotten home all right, then she drifted off to sleep.

When someone poked her roughly in the shoulder, the breakfast room had grown shadowy. Jillian sat up, squinting around blearily. She found her grandmother standing next to the table, looking down on her with her hands on her hips. "What time is it?"

"Time for you to head up to bed," Bertie said. "Laura Lee took the information for a missing person's report, so Alice was finally willing to leave. Then we all cleaned up. There's nothing for you to do but go to bed. I'll check on you through the night."

Jillian gently shook her head at that. "I don't think you should worry about that." Then she smiled a little. "By the way, the ER doctor apparently went to school with you and Aunt Cornelia. He seemed to think you were a real cutie when you were young."

Bertie shrugged. "I was. Now I'm a tired, old woman. I'm going to bed, but I'll set an alarm every couple of hours to look in on you."

Jillian snorted. "You're not old." She looked around the room. "Did anyone ever find Chess?"

"No," Bertie said. "Possum is missing as well. I practically had to strong-arm Cornelia to get her to give up the search. I reminded her that 'Raymond' was well able to look out for himself.'"

Jillian raised her eyebrows. "Raymond? You called the cat Raymond? I thought you didn't believe in supporting Aunt Cornelia's delusions."

"I was desperate. And now I'm desperately tired. I'm going upstairs, and you should too. At least you can sleep through the night, even if I can't."

"I will head upstairs in a few minutes," Jillian promised. "I might eat something first."

Bertie nodded, then left the room.

Jillian stood and gently prodded the bandage on her head. The lump underneath was tender, but her head didn't pound as it had earlier. Apparently her nap had helped, though it left her with a distinctly sore back, unless that came from falling down the stairs with a mortician on top of her.

Jillian opened the fridge and stared inside, blinking against the bright light in the shadowy kitchen. All the leftover reception food crowded the shelves, but she rooted around until she found a container of yogurt. After retrieving a spoon from the clean dishes in the dishwasher, she walked across the room to the windows in the breakfast area.

Stepping outside, she let the cool shadows in the yard soothe her head, though she half-expected to see some ghastly haint flitting around in search of someone to terrorize. Instead, she only saw the pale glow of the solar lights marking the paths into the back garden. She was glad to see someone had turned off the lights woven into the small trees, or else they had never been turned on, since the reception had never really happened.

"What's going on?" she whispered into the quiet around her. How was it that her first attempt at a grand event had gone so spectacularly wrong? Not that she could blame herself for the rehearsal apparition or for the disappearance of the groom. All of that was simple bad luck on the part of poor Alice Blackwater.

Poor Alice. Unlucky in love. Of course, Jillian had spectacularly bad luck herself. After all, she'd fallen in love in high school, only to have her boyfriend run off with the most obnoxious girl in the school, sending her fleeing across the country with a broken heart. She'd thought she'd fallen in love when she'd lived in California, only to find that her fiancé turned out to be an embezzler. She'd come home in time to be suspected of murder, and when she'd gotten that settled and turned her attention to work on the house, she'd been wrapped up in another murder.

"Honestly," she whispered, "I should be glad no one has turned up dead." With a sigh, she crossed the room and tossed the empty yogurt container in the trash. All this thinking was depressing her. She'd be better off in bed.

She wandered through the dark downstairs, intending to check the front doors before heading up to bed. In the foyer, she saw the French chairs were still there, though someone had pushed them against the walls. Jillian wrinkled her nose. They could probably keep the smaller chair in the foyer, but two was too much clutter.

She hefted the chair and hauled it toward the door to her office. She'd store it in there, completing the storage-room look she seemed to be shooting for with her office decor. The chair was heavier than she'd expected, but she didn't dare put it down and push it as the noise might wake Bertie or Cornelia, and she knew they wouldn't consider moving furniture to be the proper definition of taking it easy.

The office wasn't as dark as Jillian expected. Not only had she apparently left the lamp on at her desk, but she'd also left the laptop running. She set the French chair in the corner and walked over to shut down the computer. Wincing at the brightness of the backlit computer screen, she noticed that she had unread e-mail and decided to skim them before shutting down.

The first e-mail was from Mrs. Blackwater. *This should be cheery*, she thought. Mrs. Blackwater began the e-mail by listing the ways in which she felt Jillian's event planning had been less than acceptable, and Jillian had visions of not being able to pay all the bills she'd racked up during the wedding preparation. But at the bottom of the e-mail, Mrs. Blackwater announced that although she was not happy with Jillian's work, her family had insisted that the Blackwaters honor their commitment, and so she would be dropping a check by the bakery on Monday morning.

As much as Jillian was pleased to know she was going to get paid, she wished the woman had decided to mail the check, since she doubted any interaction with her would be uplifting.

Clicking out of Mrs. Blackwater's e-mail, Jillian looked at the only other e-mail in the inbox. It was clearly spam since the sender was someone calling themselves "Spirit of Vengeance" and the message had no subject line. With no interest in whatever the spammer hoped to sell her, Jillian intended to simply delete the e-mail, but she clicked to open it instead. To her shock, she saw the e-mail wasn't attempting to sell her anything. Instead, the words fairly well screamed from the screen.

Don't think there won't be repercussions for what you decided to do. If you want to survive, you'll stick to your own business!

9

Though sleep didn't come easily after Jillian found the threatening e-mail, she woke Sunday morning feeling surprisingly refreshed, even if she was a little sore. She took a deep breath, and the faint smell of bacon made her stomach growl. She must be the last one up if Bertie was already cooking Sunday breakfast.

She found her grandmother at the counter, turning crisp bacon on the electric griddle. Nearby, two cats sat side by side, watching every move. "I see the wayward cats have returned," Jillian said. "Don't you think we should put Chess into the carrier?"

At the counter, Cornelia poured Jillian a glass of orange juice and handed it to her. "No. It's not fair to cage the poor dear when we can't return her until after church anyway."

"Not after church," Bertie said. "Monday will be soon enough."

"Still, it seems we ought to corral her somehow," Jillian said.

"No worries," Bertie said. "We can round them up again. Bacon has always been Possum's kryptonite. That's the way I get him into the carrier for vet visits, and apparently Chess has the same weakness."

"Fine, though I should let Alice Blackwater know so she has one less thing to worry about."

"All taken care of," Bertie said. "I texted her when the cats showed up. She texted back that she would get Chess on Monday."

"You sent a text?" Jillian gawked at her grandmother. It wasn't that she doubted that Bertie *could* send a text. It was that she knew her grandmother despised texting, claiming it was proof of the demise of civilization.

Her grandmother turned a laser glare toward Jillian. "I'm perfectly capable."

"I know. I know." She looked around the kitchen. "What are we having with the bacon?"

"Omelets. I already cut up some bell peppers and mushrooms. As soon as I'm done with this bacon, I'll switch over."

"I can do them," Jillian suggested. Actually, she wasn't sure. When she lived alone she used to whip up scrambled eggs with veggies for supper sometimes, but she hadn't quite mastered the beautiful, fluffy omelets her grandmother regularly made.

"You sit down." Cornelia walked around the counter and ushered Jillian to the breakfast table by the arm. "We haven't forgotten that you're supposed to be resting. And don't think we didn't notice the missing chair in the foyer this morning. I'm sure it didn't march itself into your office."

"It looked horrible in the foyer."

Bertie pointed at Jillian with her spatula. "You will rest for the next few days, or we'll lock you in your room like a Gothic heroine."

If her hunger hadn't distracted her, Jillian would have put up more of a fight. Instead, she sat at the breakfast table and watched her grandmother cook with the same rapt attention as Possum and Chess. The omelets and bacon were worth the wait, and soon, she was happily full and feeling better about the world.

"Do you have a hat I can borrow?" she asked Cornelia as she dabbed at her mouth with her napkin. "I need to cover up this bandage for church."

"Are you sure you should go?" Cornelia asked. "Maybe you should stay home with your feet up."

That did sound lovely, but Bertie chipped in quickly, "Of course she should go! Attending church *is* restful."

"It was much more restful when we were teenagers," Cornelia said with a light laugh. She leaned closer to Jillian and lowered her voice, as if passing on a secret. "The pastor was elderly and spoke in the most perfect monotone. I napped through more than one sermon."

"Well, I did not," Bertie snapped.

"Bertie!" Cornelia said with a chuckle. "I distinctly remember Mother prodding you when you started snoring one Sunday."

Bertie crossed her arms over her chest. "I had a cold. That doesn't count."

"At any rate," Jillian said, before the teasing could escalate into a full-fledged argument, "I intend to stay awake, but I still need a hat if I can borrow one."

"Of course you can," Cornelia said. "Come along now, and I'll loan you one." She hopped up, and Jillian rose to follow her. She paused for a moment, suddenly remembering the threatening e-mail from the night before and considering whether she should tell her grandmother about it. She shook off the idea. Bertie wouldn't be impressed by a vague threat from an anonymous source and would probably scold her for even thinking about it.

"Coming?" Cornelia asked.

"Of course." Jillian followed her great-aunt out of the room. To her amusement, she noticed that Cornelia "accidentally" dropped scraps of bacon in front of Possum and Chess as she walked by. The cats gobbled up the scraps and then fell in line behind Jillian, so they made a little parade up the stairs to the second floor.

The morning light coming through the stained glass dome above the stairs touched Cornelia's hair, turning the blonde strands golden and giving her tiny great-aunt an almost angelic look. When they got to Cornelia's room, it made Jillian smile. Although Bertie's bedroom downstairs was meticulously neat, almost military, Cornelia's room could be better described as controlled chaos, with shelves cluttered with knickknacks and every surface filled with her aunt's personal treasures.

Cornelia waved toward a tall coat tree where hats hung from every hook. "I don't know which dress you intend to wear, but I think the pale straw hat with the sage ribbon would look nice with your hair.

"As long as it covers up the bandage, it doesn't have to make much of a fashion statement," Jillian said. She took the straw hat from the hook and perched it on her head. It had to sit at a jaunty angle to cover the bandage completely, which gave Jillian a saucy air and made her smile. "This should do. I think I have a dress that will go with it."

"Good choice," Cornelia said. "By the way, I had a dream last night, and I wanted to tell you about it without Bertie around. She pooh-poohs things like that."

Jillian almost groaned. It was one of Cornelia's dreams that had propelled them into event planning. Well, to be fair, it probably only helped propel them; Jillian had been strongly in favor of the idea too. "What did you dream?"

"I dreamt about Raymond. I always dream about Raymond when I get a message," her aunt said. "He was wrestling an alligator, and he told me that you should be careful of the swamp."

For an instant, the image of her short, mild-mannered great-uncle wrestling an alligator filled her head, and it was all Jillian could do not to giggle, which she knew would offend her aunt, who considered her late husband quite manly. Finally, she managed to choke out a response. "I'll be careful."

Cornelia nodded, clearly happy to have carried the warning; then she shooed Jillian out of the room to change for church. As Jillian left, both cats were sprawled on the bed, watching Cornelia closely as if expecting her to drop more bacon at any moment.

Jillian rooted through the tall cherry wardrobe in her room and found a fitted linen wrap dress with pastel flowers embroidered down the front and around the hem. She slipped into it and was pleased to see it was a nice match with the hat. The fitted style showed off her figure while looking completely appropriate for church as well. She matched the dress with some nice sage flats that almost perfectly matched the ribbon on the hat.

"Not bad after a tumble down the stairs," Jillian said as she winked at her rakish look in the mirror.

Though Pastor Keith was anything but dull, Jillian was still rather proud not to have nodded off in church since she realized she wasn't quite as recovered from her fall as she'd thought. She noticed Hunter was nowhere to be seen in the congregation and felt a wave of guilt, assuming his injury had kept him home.

After the service, Jillian whispered to Bertie, "I'm going out to the car. You and Cornelia take as long as you want, but I'm a little tired."

Bertie peered at her closely. "You do look peaked. But remember that the Sweetie Pies meeting is early today to accommodate Maudie's need to escape from the house before her husband's baseball game comes on."

"Oh, right," Jillian said as guilt washed over her. The Sweetie Pies had done so much, from helping with the remodel to working at both the rehearsal dinner and the wedding, but she didn't feel up to a meeting.

"I can take you home."

Jillian turned to see Savannah walking up the aisle. Her friend looked lovely in a blue-gray silky blouse and white skirt. "I don't want to make you late for the meeting," Jillian said.

"If I'm late, it won't be by much," Savannah said cheerfully. "I don't mind. I'll feel I did my good deed for the day if you get some rest."

"Then it's settled," Bertie said with her usual air of having the last word in everything. "I'll see you at home after the meeting. Wanda Jean is in charge of the refreshments this time, and she's sure to bring her orange pound cake. I'll bring you home some."

Jillian smiled fondly at her grandmother. Though she was endlessly bossy, she also always made Jillian feel loved. "Thanks, Bertie."

Jillian and Savannah wove through the congregation and slipped outside. The day was painfully bright, waking up Jillian's sluggish headache again, so she slipped a pair of sunglasses from her purse and put them on.

"With the glasses and the hat, you look like a movie star," Savannah said.

"Hardly, after a difficult night," Jillian said. "I woke up feeling well, but my headache is back."

"Well, you *did* fall down a flight of stairs with a man on top of you," Savannah said.

"You make that sound far racier than it was," Jillian said. "And I noticed Hunter wasn't at church. I feel terrible considering Possum knocked him over."

Savannah laughed lightly. "And he feels terrible for knocking you down. I could take you by his place, and you two could have a guilt-off."

"No thanks," Jillian said, then had an odd thought, remembering her promise to Alice. "But we might make one quick stop, if you don't mind."

"Sure, where to?" Savannah asked as they reached her car. "The drugstore?"

Jillian shook her head and pulled her phone out of her purse. Running through her contacts where she had information on all the members of the wedding party, she quickly found what she needed. "I want to run by Gordon Liddell's apartment. I promised Alice I'd look into it, so I want to be able to say I did *something*."

"What if he's there?" Savannah asked as she opened the driver's side door.

"Then I'll probably call him a few well-chosen names for upsetting her and making a mess of my first professional event. Then I'll tell him to call Alice." Jillian carefully lifted the hat from her head and tossed it onto the backseat. It was too warm for a hat, and the ache in her head was getting worse.

The old brick apartment house where Gordon lived was actually not far from the church. Despite her tough talk about what she would say to Gordon, she hoped he wasn't there. She intended her visit to be more of a symbolic gesture than any real investigation. She still thought finding missing persons was more of a police matter than anything she should be doing. But Alice had gotten her mother to agree to pay the wedding bills, so Jillian owed her something.

Gordon's apartment building sat across the street from one of Moss Hollow's larger parks. The old Craftsman-style brick building had been built in the 1920s, and when it was renovated into upscale apartments, the exterior stayed as original as possible. The two-story building housed four apartments, each with a generous brick porch facing the park. The building's front double doors matched the French doors that led out from the first-floor apartments and onto their porches on either side.

"I remember when the historical society was helping to restore this building, but I haven't been inside," Savannah said as they headed up the walk to the front door of the building. When they walked in and noticed the worn hardwood floor of the foyer with its dark, well-polished finish, Savannah whispered, "Nice."

Together, Jillian and Savannah headed up the stairs to the second-floor apartments and found Gordon's door ajar. "Louis Blackwater said his friend locked the apartment when he left," Jillian whispered.

Savannah stepped close to the door and peeked in the crack. "It's not locked now."

Jillian rapped on the door with her knuckles, and it swung open farther. "Gordon? Are you here? It's Jillian Green. Alice asked me to come by."

When they didn't get an answer, Jillian and Savannah exchanged looks, then gently pushed the door open and stepped inside. The apartment looked as if a small tornado had passed through, turning over furniture and destroying everything in its path.

"It seems to me that Louis's friend would have mentioned this destruction," Jillian said.

"Yeah, maybe we aren't the only people looking for Gordon." Jillian nodded. "Or for something he has."

Savannah looked at her, wide-eyed. "I think it's time to call 911."

10

"You're right," Jillian said. "And we will, but what if Gordon is in here somewhere hurt? He could die while we wait for someone to respond to the call."

"We should still call before we look," Savannah said. "So they'll be on the way." She pulled her phone from her pocket and groaned. "I don't get service in here."

Jillian checked her phone and shook her head. "Me either. Someone told me once that older buildings sometimes act like a Faraday cage because of all the metal in the construction."

"This building is brick," Savannah said.

Jillian shrugged. "I'm not an engineer. One of us needs to go outside to make the call."

"We should both go," Savannah said. "I don't want to leave you in here alone."

"I'll be fine. I'm going to do a quick look for Gordon, then I'll wait out in the hall. My guess is that whoever tore up this place is long gone."

To her relief, Savannah didn't argue. As she listened to her friend's footsteps on the stairs, Jillian began looking around the small apartment. Though not exactly roomy, the place was attractive, with original hardwood floors and a neat fireplace in the main room. The Craftsman-style mantel and subway-tile firebox surround looked original, as did some of the lighting fixtures.

She didn't spend much time admiring, focusing instead on peeking into any corner where a body might lie. The sofa had been overturned near the fireplace, and Jillian crouched down to look under it. She saw no sign of Gordon, though she did see a scattering of torn papers. Jillian fished out one of the scraps and looked at it. It was a piece of a photograph. *Why would someone tear up a photo?* Impulsively, she gathered up all the pieces she could easily reach and shoved them into her purse.

With no more hiding spots available in the main room, she checked the kitchen, where the cupboard doors hung open and the contents had been emptied onto the floor, making a mess she chose not to wade into. The fridge stood open, so it was obvious Gordon wasn't stuffed in there.

She walked down a narrow hall and peeked into the bathroom. To her surprise, the shower curtain wasn't pulled down. Instead, it neatly obscured the tub. *Gordon could be lying dead in the tub.* Jillian swallowed the lump that lodged in her throat. In movies, a body in a bathtub was never very nice to look at. Still, it wasn't impossible that Gordon was in the tub, alive but bleeding and in need of help while she stood there imagining old horror movies. Giving herself a mental shake, she squared her shoulders and walked across the pale tile floor. The thick vinyl of the shower curtain felt sticky against her fingers as she grabbed it and wrenched it open.

The tub was empty. Jillian nearly whimpered in relief. She hurried on to the bedroom where the bedcovers were drawn up over a body-shaped lump. More horror-movie images tried to wedge into her head, but she refused to stop and merely crossed the room and pulled back the comforter. Underneath, someone had piled the contents of the dresser drawers before pulling the covers over them. She scanned the pile of clothes and shoes but saw nothing that resembled clues. She walked around the bed to check the floor. It was a mess of broken things swept from the top of the dresser, but there was no body. Whoever had been in the apartment certainly seemed angry, judging by the destruction.

Before leaving the room, she glanced toward the mirror over the dresser. A long crack ran diagonally across the mirror, but the most interesting thing wasn't the crack, but the writing scrawled near the bottom edge in blood red: *Killer!*

Jillian looked closely at the irregular writing. What she'd taken for blood looked more like cosmetics now that she saw it closer—lipstick probably. Gordon didn't seem the red-lipstick sort, so maybe the person who trashed the apartment was a woman. But what did the message mean? Was it an accusation or a signature?

"Jillian! Are you all right?"

Savannah's voice wasn't close, and Jillian suspected she was standing outside the apartment in the hallway. "I'm coming!" she called, then snapped a photo of the message with her phone.

Once she joined Savannah in the hall, she quickly filled her in on what she'd found.

"I can't believe you took the pieces of photo," Savannah whispered fiercely. "Isn't that tampering with evidence?"

"Once I look at it, I'll turn it in, I promise," Jillian said. "But I promised Alice I'd look into Gordon's disappearance."

"You didn't promise to do something illegal while you're at it," Savannah said.

"Illegal-ish," Jillian said. She wasn't sure what the penalty for picking up the photo scraps might be. With a sigh, she walked over to a small table under the window at the end of the hallway. She laid out the scraps and quickly put them together. Though several pieces were still missing, it was clear the photo was of Gordon with his arm around the shoulders of another man. She didn't recognize the second man, though something about it looked vaguely familiar. Of course, the fact that part of his face was still missing could be obscuring identification. She snapped a picture of the assembled photo, then reached into the apartment and threw in the scraps.

"There, no more missing evidence," she said.

"You know your fingerprints are going to be on those now," Savannah said.

"It's not going to be a secret that I went in there," Jillian answered. "After all, I was trying to save Gordon."

Before Savannah could respond, they froze at sounds coming from downstairs. Someone was coming through the door and tromping up the stairs. To Jillian's surprise, and definitely not to her delight, Deputy Sheriff Goodman Jones, known locally as Gooder, appeared at the top of the stairs. The tall, broad-shouldered man shook his head as soon as he spotted her. "I wondered how long it would be before you were involved in another suspicious circumstance."

"I'm not really involved," Jillian protested. "I just happened to find the door open and the apartment trashed." She pointed inside. "I went in to look for Gordon, in case he was attacked and bleeding somewhere, but no one is in there. The place is all torn up. You'll find some scraps of photo. I touched them, but they're all inside."

The deputy narrowed his eyes. "Why doesn't it surprise me that you're already tampering with a crime scene?"

"She wasn't tampering, Gooder," Savannah said loyally, if not altogether correctly. "If Gordon was in there injured, he could have died waiting for help."

"Fine." He pointed at the side of Jillian's head. "Who bashed you in the head? Is it related to this?"

"First, I want to make it clear that there was no breaking. Just entering. The door was ajar when we got here," Jillian said. "Second, I fell down the stairs at Belle Haven because of our cat. And I'm pretty sure Possum isn't the one who trashed Gordon's apartment."

The deputy held up both hands. "Settle down. I had to ask.

Now, you two stay here while I check out the apartment. I may have more questions once I'm done."

While they waited for Gooder to finish his search, Jillian wished she had someplace to sit down. Her head was really beginning to throb. *This is what I get for skipping out on the Sweetie Pies meeting*, she thought glumly. *I could be eating cake right now.*

"Do you think we're in any trouble?" Savannah asked quietly.

Jillian shook her head, then winced, realizing she'd reached a point in the headache where the less she moved her head, the better. "Gooder Jones just likes to give me a hard time."

"*Me* give *you* a hard time?" he squawked, stepping through the apartment doorway. "You're the one who doesn't know how to leave things alone."

"And you're the one acting as if I didn't play an important part in putting killers behind bars," Jillian said.

"You're lucky you survived the process," he snapped, then crossed his arms over his chest and stared down at her in a clear attempt to intimidate. "And speaking of killers, I assume you saw the message."

"I did," Jillian said, imitating the deputy's stance and glaring right back at him. She was tired and annoyed, and she wasn't in the mood for Gooder's games.

"What's the story on this guy?" Gooder glanced down at his notepad. "Gordon Liddell. You know him?"

"Slightly," Jillian said, losing some of her defiant stance. "We were hosting a wedding at Belle Haven this weekend. Gordon was to be the groom, but he never showed. I promised the bride I'd try to find him, so I came by here after church and found what you saw inside."

"You know of any reason someone might accuse him of murder?" Gooder asked.

Jillian shook her head, then winced again. "No. Can we be done soon? I need to go home."

He narrowed his eyes at her. "You're not keeping anything from me?"

"No."

He looked closely at Savannah, giving her the same hard stare, but she simply smiled back. "I'm only the driver."

"Fine. Go home. But I may have more questions after I have some techs go over the room."

"You have techs?" Jillian asked, surprised.

"This isn't Mayberry," he snapped. "We're professionals."

She thought of a couple remarks but swallowed them. She really did want to go home. "I hope you find him," she said softly, then turned away and headed down the stairs. Savannah followed along behind her.

"Are you going to call Alice?" Savannah asked when they got outside.

"I suppose I should. It will be better hearing about the break-in from someone she knows, plus I can assure her I didn't see any sign that Gordon was hurt."

"I wonder where he is," Savannah said.

"That does seem to be the big question." Jillian stopped when they reached the sidewalk. A small parking lot ran along one side of the apartment house. Her gaze swept over the lot, and she pointed at a small, dark-blue sedan. "I think that's Gordon's car."

"His car is in the lot, but he's gone," Savannah said. "That doesn't seem good."

Jillian walked closer to the car. She'd only seen Gordon's car from a distance, but it certainly looked like it. Remembering Savannah's earlier remark about fingerprints, she reached into her purse and pulled out the snow-white handkerchief her grandmother felt all well-bred Southern women should carry to church. She used it to try the driver's door and found it unlocked.

"Oh, no," Savannah said. "You know you should leave that alone."

"I probably should," Jillian agreed as she bent to peek into the car, then gasped. A smear of red ran across the top of the steering wheel. "Actually," she whispered, "I think you're absolutely right. We should leave this alone."

After letting Gooder know about the car, Jillian and Savannah left so Gooder could conduct his investigation in peace. Jillian went home and spent the rest of Sunday resting in her room at Belle Haven with the curtains drawn and the lights off.

Both Bertie and Cornelia frowned at her as she walked down to the breakfast table the next morning, and Jillian was struck by how much the twins looked alike in that moment. Their very different temperaments and fashion choices often made it easy to forget they were identical twins.

"You shouldn't be up. The doctor told you to rest," Cornelia insisted.

"I rested all afternoon and most of the evening yesterday," Jillian said. "I'm amazed I was able to sleep at all last night after napping half the day."

"I notice you managed to find trouble before you came home yesterday," Bertie said.

Jillian hadn't told anyone about visiting Gordon's apartment, and she couldn't imagine Savannah calling to squeal on her. "Where did you hear that?"

"Don't be a goose," Bertie said. "We have a deputy in the Sweetie Pies. Did you think Laura Lee wouldn't hear about your antics and pass them on?"

For a moment, Jillian was disappointed to think Laura Lee would rat her out, then she realized what must have happened. "She got the call during the meeting, didn't she?" Jillian asked. "And you badgered her until she told you what it was about."

Her grandmother gave a delicate sniff. "I do not badger people.

Laura Lee naturally told me about the incident once I reminded her that you *are* my granddaughter."

Since Jillian had never been good at resisting Bertie when she was in her most bossy mode, she decided not to be miffed at Laura Lee. "I was making good on a promise to Alice Blackwater, a promise I was blackmailed into making. She's pretty good at being manipulative. Are you sure she's not a relative?"

"Hardly." Bertie took a deep sip of her coffee, giving Jillian a chance to sit down, grab a slice of toast, and slather it with butter and homemade strawberry jam.

"Do you know where Alice's cat is?" Jillian asked Cornelia.

Her aunt nibbled delicately at the corner of a slice of toast and made Jillian wait until she'd chewed the morsel thoroughly and swallowed. "Chess is in my room. I'll put her in the carrier after breakfast, but do not make the poor darling sit in the carrier all morning."

"Josi Rosenschein watched Chess at the library last time," Jillian said. "I'll pop in and leave the cat with her. The library won't be open yet, but Josi always comes in early, so I'm pretty sure she'll let me in."

Cornelia nodded in approval and returned her attention to her eggs and toast.

"Since you're resting, you can help Maggie up front with customers," Bertie said.

Jillian stared at her grandmother for a moment on the off chance that Bertie was kidding. *Does she really think dealing with the customers at The Chocolate Shoppe Bakery is a form of resting?*

Bertie didn't seem to notice Jillian's stare and simply forked scrambled eggs into her mouth. With a sigh, Jillian bit into her toast and crunched in annoyance.

Within the hour, Jillian was hauling the heavy cat carrier down the sidewalk from the bakery to the library. The tall brick building that housed the Moss Hollow Library had housed Cooper's Pharmacy when Jillian was a little girl, and she had fond memories of sitting on the tall stools and sipping milk shakes with Bertie, in between scoldings for spinning on the stool. Now, the building held a different and far less fattening treat with the small-town library.

As she'd expected, the front door of the library was locked, but she knocked on the glass until Josi came to the door. The librarian pointed at the sign with the library's hours. Jillian replied by pointing at the cat carrier and looking as woeful as she could manage.

The librarian turned the lock and cracked the door. "Same cat?"

Jillian nodded. "Chess escaped from her mistress before the wedding, and I need to return her. Could you look after her again? It should be the same as last time."

"I heard about the wedding." Josi's eyes sparkled with mirth. "Apparently Moss Hollow's mortician fell hard for you." She giggled at her own joke.

Jillian felt a tug of guilt at not calling Hunter to see how he was recovering after the accident. She smiled at Josi's joke, then gently pushed the carrier toward her. "Can I count on you to look after Chess for a little while?"

"Sure, she'll be good company," Josi said. "I'm alone until our volunteer comes." She sighed deeply. "Budget cuts mean I have to tag-team with our other librarian on Mondays and Wednesdays, which can be challenging sometimes."

Jillian smiled sympathetically while managing to hand off the cat. "I need to dash back to the bakery before Bertie comes looking for me. I'm on front duty this morning, and we'll be opening soon."

"Have fun," Josi said as Jillian saw her set the cat carrier on the floor beside her to relock the door.

Jillian gave her one more wave through the glass, then hurried back to the bakery. She managed to get to the front door of the bakery at the same moment that Bertie stood on the other side, flipping the door sign to *Open*.

"Maggie is running late," Bertie grumbled. "That girl needs a new car."

Jillian considered reminding Bertie that they didn't pay Maggie nearly enough for her to buy a new car, but since Jillian knew they couldn't afford to give the young woman a raise, she decided to keep the remark to herself. Instead, she quickly crossed the room and put on one of the crisp white aprons with *The Chocolate Shoppe Bakery* embroidered in red across the bib. They only wore the fancy aprons when they were working the front. The work aprons for the kitchen lacked both the crispness and the embroidery but covered up a larger area of their clothes.

The hungry customers must have sensed the flipping of the sign because they began to stream in almost the moment Jillian got her apron tied. For over an hour, she was too busy to think about anything but bear claws and cinnamon rolls as she packed pastries in boxes and slipped them into bags for the steady stream of people.

She was so caught up in the process that she didn't see Hunter until he was standing on the other side of the counter. He gave her a smile that made her insides flutter, a feeling she promptly squashed. "How's your arm?" she asked.

He raised the arm slightly in the sling. "Healing but still a little sore. It made tying my tie an adventure this morning."

Jillian winced. "Sorry about that."

"How about we make a deal?" Hunter asked. "You stop feeling guilty about the cats, and I'll stop feeling guilty about falling on you. How's your head?"

"Sore, but better. Honestly, the worst part has been not being able to wash my hair and risk getting the stitches wet."

"You look lovely to me," he said with a smile.

Jillian felt the flutters return but merely thanked him for the compliment. "So what can I get you this morning?"

He ordered a selection of pastries. "Savannah is at the office working on the books this morning, so I need a few extras. Do you happen to know her favorite?"

"Apple fritters," Jillian said. "Savannah has always loved cinnamon and apples."

"Excellent, let me have two of those." He watched as Jillian loaded the pastries in a box. "She told me about your adventure yesterday. It sounds like a situation you should stay far away from."

Jillian eyed him sharply. There was some part of her that always reacted whenever anyone told her not to do something. She knew it wasn't her best trait, but it was a hard one to suppress. "I'll be careful," she promised.

She was distracted from further conversation when Maggie practically flew through the front door of the bakery, flinging apologies for being so late. She wove around the line of clients and slipped behind the counter, grabbing an apron from the shelf under the cash register. "I had to wait for my brother to come get my car going," she said. "I'm so sorry."

Jillian patted the girl's arm. "It's all right. We all have car trouble sometimes." She handed the box of pastries over the counter to Hunter and collected his money.

Behind him, an elderly man in slightly grubby overalls grumbled, "It's about time." He stepped up to the counter and shook a finger at Jillian. "You should manage your love life on your own time, not when customers are waiting."

Jillian blinked at him in shock. "I beg your pardon?"

"Work first, flirt later," he demanded.

Jillian sputtered for a moment, her fingers clenching into fists, shocked that anyone would think she was flirting with Hunter Greyson when she'd simply been filling his order.

Something in Jillian's stance must have alarmed Maggie as the young woman gently eased closer and smiled brightly at the old man. "What can I get for you, Mr. Ward?"

Jillian backed away from the counter so she wouldn't give in to the urge to throw a cheese danish at the man. What happened to gracious Southern manners? She considered slipping into the kitchen so she could stomp around and rant for a minute, but Alice Blackwater chose that moment to burst through the front door with nearly as much rush as Maggie had shown.

"Excuse me," Jillian whispered to Maggie. "I'll be right back." She slipped out from behind the counter and walked over to meet Alice, waving her toward one of the tables and chairs that were still empty.

Alice nodded and sat down, immediately rooting through her purse. She pulled out a slip of paper and passed it across the table to Jillian. "I volunteered to carry the check to you today since I needed to pick up Chess anyway. Mother wanted to do it, but I figured you didn't really need the conflict."

"I appreciate that so very much. Your cat is at the library again. The librarian was kind enough to look after her so that she wouldn't have to be cooped up in the carrier," Jillian said fervently as she picked up the check and fingered it nervously. "I assume you've heard from Deputy Jones?"

Alice's eyes went shiny with unshed tears, but then she sat up straighter and cleared her throat. "Yes. He mentioned that you're the one who discovered the apartment door open. I appreciate you trying to find Gordon." Her voice choked, and she took a moment to recover before adding, "I hope you'll keep looking."

"Miss Blackwater . . . Alice," Jillian said gently, "after what the deputy found at the apartment yesterday, he cannot possibly think Gordon simply left. The deputy will look for Gordon. I think it's time to let the professionals do their job."

"I have no faith in professionals." Alice practically spat out the last word. She laced her fingers together in front of her on the table. "The professionals certainly never found Jacob, and they've had more than a year."

Jillian didn't know what to say to that, so she merely fidgeted with the check, trying to think of another way to deflect the pressure Alice was putting on her.

"Do you know what Deputy Jones suggested?" Alice asked, her voice thin and tight.

Jillian shook her head.

"He said it was interesting that this is the second fiancé I've *misplaced*," Alice said. "He even confiscated all of my lipstick to compare with some message they found on a mirror. He wouldn't even tell me what the message said." She leaned forward over the table. "Did you see it?"

"It was a crime scene," Jillian said, carefully avoiding the question. "I was focused on making sure Gordon wasn't in the apartment, injured." Then she had a thought. "I did see a photo, torn up on the floor. I took a picture with my phone." She called up the picture and showed it to Alice. "Do you know the second man?"

Alice took the phone from her and looked at the screen for a long moment. Then she nodded. "I know this photo. Gordon kept it on the fireplace mantel. That's him with Jacob, taken in the swamp at Duvall Island."

"Alice, do you know why Jacob went to Duvall Island?" Jillian asked. "Apparently he went there a lot, and clearly Gordon went with him at least once. Were they fishing or hunting?"

Alice shook her head. "Neither. Jacob was doing research for a book."

"A book? About Duvall Island?" Jillian asked.

"Not exactly," Alice answered. "It was about Okefenokee ghost stories, but Jacob said that Duvall Island was some kind of focal point for the stories because of the giants."

"Giants?" Jillian asked.

Alice nodded and reluctantly handed the phone back to Jillian. "Years ago, the swampers who built a homestead on Duvall Island dug up a whole pit filled with skeletons of giant men. Visitors to the island and some of the volunteers who work there supposedly see the ghosts of those giants regularly. Jacob was going to make them the focal point of the book."

"Did Jacob want to be a writer?" Jillian said.

Alice shrugged. "Sort of. This was going to be his first book. Mostly he ran a little antique shop, but I know his heart wasn't in it. If it was, he wouldn't have spent so many weekends off on investigations. He was a member of the Lowlands Paranormal Investigators."

"Paranormal Investigators?" Jillian echoed.

"Ghost hunters," Alice said, then her eyes widened as an idea came to her. "Maybe that's why he showed up at the rehearsal dinner." She managed a small smile. "He wasn't trying to scare me. He wanted to show me that ghosts are real."

As unrealistic as Jillian thought that was, she didn't have the heart to comment as she looked into Alice's hopeful face. "I suspect there is more going on here than ghosts. I don't believe ghosts ransacked Gordon's apartment."

"No, Jacob's ghost wouldn't do that. He and Gordon were friends."

Not to mention the ridiculous idea of a ghost carrying around a lipstick. Jillian folded her hands on the table in front of her. "I'll admit, I want to know what's going on here, but this has become a police investigation, and it would be illegal for me to interfere."

Alice's hopeful look darkened. "From what I've heard, that

didn't keep you from poking around when Nadine Belmont was murdered."

Because I was a suspect! Jillian's knuckles whitened as she tightened the grip of her clenched hands, to keep her annoyance from showing in her face. "Those were special circumstances."

"So are these. You promised to help. You may have Mother's check, but you don't have her goodwill. If you're wanting to continue your business, it's a good idea not to upset me."

"I can see you're already upset," Jillian said gently.

"You don't have a clue about how upset I can get."

The resemblance between Alice and her mother reflected in more than her looks. "Are you threatening me?" Jillian asked.

"Sure," Alice said. "I'll do whatever I have to. I want my fiancé back. And you're either part of the solution or you're part of the problem. And my mother has spent many years showing me what to do about problems."

The bakery fell unnaturally quiet, the patrons obviously shocked by Alice Blackwater's loud threat. Jillian wondered, not for the first time, how she got herself into these kinds of situations. She wasn't looking for trouble. She wanted a nice, normal life of helping her grandmother and occasionally burning a few brownies.

Is that too much to ask?

"I honestly don't know what to tell you, Miss Blackwater," Jillian said quietly, hoping her choice of formal title for her client would get them back on a professional footing and end the bizarre turn the conversation had taken. "I honestly have no idea how I would look for your fiancé. I don't know him or much about him."

Alice sat back, and her intense look softened. "I've thought about that. I think you're going to have to go to the swamp."

"The swamp!" Jillian squeaked.

"It's where this all started, and it's clearly what he was trying to tell me at the rehearsal dinner," Alice said. "And now we have this torn photo, taken in the swamp at Duvall Island. Going to the swamp is the obvious next step."

"Do I look like someone who wanders around in a swamp?" Jillian asked. She pointed to her head. "Plus, I have stitches, and I'm sure I saw a nature documentary once that said open wounds in the swamp are very dangerous. The person in the documentary got some kind of horrific parasite that way."

Alice leaned forward again, narrowing her eyes. "So put a bigger bandage on it. I'll expect to get regular reports on your efforts. E-mail will be fine. You don't have to call. But don't test me on this. I *am* my mother's daughter. I can assure you of that."

Jillian felt slightly dazed as Alice stood and straightened her shoulders.

"I believe you said Chess is at the library?"

Jillian nodded mutely.

"Excellent. I'll go pick her up. I've missed her, though she's terribly naughty for running off. Thank you for your time. I'll look forward to your first report." At that, Alice turned on her heel and marched out of the bakery.

For a moment, Jillian stared after her, wondering again how she got into these things. She couldn't think of a worse idea than poking around in the swamp. With a sigh, she stood and headed back behind the counter. "Can you handle things out here?" she whispered to Maggie. "If I spend anymore time at this 'restful activity,' I'm going to cry."

Maggie looked at her sympathetically. "No problem."

Jillian stepped through the doorway into the kitchen area of the bakery and gently began tucking her hair into a pink hairnet, being careful not to poke at the bandage on the side of her head, and then walked to the sink and washed her hands. She found the mindless steps soothing after her conversation with Alice.

"What are you doing back here?" Bertie demanded, shattering Jillian's soothing calm. "I thought you were going to work the front with Maggie?"

"If I have any more 'restful' front work, I am going to start slipping sedatives into the pastries," Jillian said. "I cannot imagine what made you think dealing with customers is restful."

Bertie shrugged. "I don't have any problems with them."

That's because you can be a scary, scary woman, Jillian thought, but she had enough survival instinct not to say it. "I don't seem to have your touch." She pulled the check from the Blackwaters from her apron pocket. "But I did get paid."

Bertie's face brightened. "That's good."

"Yes and no," Jillian said. "Alice Blackwater still thinks I should locate her fiancé. Actually, she probably wants me to find both the living fiancé and the dead one."

Bertie shook her head. "Sounds like the poor girl is unhinged." Bertie's gaze swept over the kitchen. "Well, since you're not going to work the front, maybe you could make a batch of triple-chocolate brownies. We're running low."

"Really?" Jillian said. "I tell you that our client wants me to track down a missing fiancé and your answer is brownies, my baking nemesis?"

"You've been awfully dramatic since you fell down and hurt your head," Bertie said. "They did check you out, right?"

"Yes, they did check me out. And I'm not being dramatic," Jillian said. "Forget it. I'll make the brownies, but if the bakery doesn't survive, don't blame me."

"Defeatist thinking never accomplished anything," Bertie called after her as Jillian stomped through the kitchen to the far prep table that held several of the "small" mixers, which were still huge compared to what most home cooks would have.

Jillian hefted one of the heavy mixing bowls from the shelf under the prep table and settled it onto the arms of the mixer. She pulled the flip file of recipes close enough to read off the ingredients and began the process of making the dark, rich brownies that had become the bane of her existence.

"What you up to over here?"

"Brownies," Jillian answered, not even turning to look at Lenora. "It was Bertie's idea. I think it's her version of endlessly shoving me back up on the horse after I fall off."

Lenora leaned against the end of the worktable and watched

Jillian chop the baking chocolate into bits that would melt smoothly with the butter. She reached out and put a hand on Jillian's arm. "Sweetie, I think that's chopped enough. What did that chocolate ever do to you?"

Jillian looked down at the finely chopped pile of dark chocolate. "I've had a rough morning."

"You've had a rough couple of days," Lenora said. "But what happened now?"

Jillian scooped up the chopped chocolate with her board scraper and dumped it into a glass bowl for melting in the microwave, since she wasn't going to try using a double boiler. Her one experience with that had burned the chocolate and flooded the floor around the cooktop. She glanced at Lenora. "Alice Blackwater thinks I should go out into the Okefenokee Swamp to look for her fiancé."

Lenora's eyes widened in alarm. "You're not going, are you?"

Jillian was surprised at the force behind the question. "I don't know. Alice clearly plans to blackmail me if I don't. We've sunk a lot of money into renovating in order to hold some events at the mansion. I'd hate to see that ruined, and maybe the bakery along with it."

"The bakery will be fine," Lenora said. "But that swamp is dangerous. I wouldn't go out there."

"Actually, the place where Alice's first fiancé disappeared is a tourist site," Jillian said. "So it's probably fairly safe, though full of mosquitoes and heat and creepy-crawlies."

"What tourist site?"

"Duvall Island," Jillian said. "I looked it up online. There's a little homestead. It's actually kind of cute."

"Nothing about Duvall Island is cute," Lenora insisted, crossing her arms over her ample bosom. "That place is crawling with haints."

Jillian groaned. "You know, I expect that kind of thing from Aunt Cornelia, but I thought you were more sensible."

"Just because I don't think your grandmother's cat is actually housing Cornelia's dead husband doesn't mean I'm going to march off into the swamps. That's a totally different thing. The stories about the swamps are old, as old as anything in the South."

Jillian snorted as she began cutting up half a stick of butter into the bowl with the baking chocolate and then stirred the mixture. "Superstitions don't become true simply because they've been repeated and believed a long time."

"They don't become false simply because you don't believe them either," Lenora said. She shook her finger at Jillian. "You best stay out of the swamp. Your grandmother needs you. You don't need to take that kind of risk."

Jillian looked directly at Lenora and saw real distress on her dark, round face. "I promise not to take any risks," she said. "Well, other than these brownies."

To Jillian's absolute shock, the brownies turned out perfectly when she pulled them from the oven slightly more than thirty minutes later. She carefully slipped a toothpick in the middle and nearly cheered when it came out with a few moist crumbs, exactly as it should.

Bertie walked over as Jillian slipped the pan into a rack to cool. She looked over the brownies and nodded. "I knew you could do it. Baking is in your blood. Maybe you needed a whack in the head to knock it loose. I'll have to remember that."

Jillian refused to let her grandmother's teasing take the edge off her success. She was so pleased with the brownies that she promised herself one after they were cut. She dusted off her hands on her apron and turned to her grandmother. "What should I do now?"

"You should go out front," Bertie said.

"No," Jillian moaned. "Can't someone else wait on customers?"

"Maggie is handling that," Bertie said. "You should go out front to see Savannah. She dropped by and is waiting for you." Bertie nodded toward the rack. "And you've earned a break. Maybe you two should go eat lunch somewhere."

Jillian almost demanded that Bertie tell her what she'd done with her real grandmother, but she decided not to antagonize the older woman while she was in a generous mood. Instead, she pulled off her apron and hairnet, and hurried out to meet Savannah.

"I've been sprung," she said as she walked around the counter. "Want to go to lunch?"

Savannah smiled. "Sounds good. I came by to see how you were doing, but I don't mind staying for lunch."

"We're not staying here," Jillian said, herding her friend toward the door. "Our sandwiches are good, but Bertie is sure to remember something she wants me to do. Let's go to Crazy Fish."

"Twice in less than a week? I didn't know you enjoyed fish that much."

Once they were outside, Jillian headed down the sidewalk toward the narrow alley that led to the back of the bakery to the small parking lot for the bakery employees. "It seemed the right choice today, since I want to talk about the swamp."

"I'm intrigued." As they stepped into the alley, Savannah looked at the row of trash cans and laughed. "You do take me to the best places."

"I'm parked back here," Jillian said, then she stopped so suddenly that Savannah nearly ran into her. "I'm sorry, I assumed

I'd be driving. I think I've grown up to be my grandmother. Are you all right with me driving?"

"Sure, saves my gas. I had to park back in the tourist lot near the historical society anyway. There was nothing available on the street."

On the drive to the restaurant, Jillian caught Savannah up on her conversation with Alice Blackwater. "She's threatening to hurt our business if I don't help."

Savannah's expression darkened. "I don't like the sound of blackmail, and I enjoy giving in to it even less."

"I think Alice is desperate," Jillian said. "That's a feeling I've had before myself. I thought I might drive down to the Okefenokee National Wildlife Refuge tomorrow. I looked it up online before I considered going there. Once you're in the park, it's not far to Duvall Island. It's a major tourist site. I can ask around about Jacob and Gordon. See if any of the park employees remember them."

"Might be interesting. Would you like some company?"

Jillian turned a quick smile toward her friend. "I was hoping you'd ask. Though I should probably warn you, apparently there are ghosts out there."

Savannah laughed. "We ain't 'fraid of no ghosts."

Jillian laughed along with her.

They soon reached the restaurant and blinked away the temporary blindness after stepping from the bright spring sunshine into the lesser lighting of the restaurant's dining room. The hostess led them around the tables, and Jillian was surprised to see she recognized the person sitting alone at one of the tables. She stopped next to the table. "Rose, right? From Quest for Beauty?"

The woman looked up from the menu she was studying. "Oh, I remember you. You were having a wedding at that lovely old mansion."

"Belle Haven, right," Jillian said. She noticed that Savannah and the hostess had stopped and were waiting. Savannah wore a slight smile, while the hostess seemed to be struggling not to look annoyed by the delay. Jillian waved toward them. "Go ahead. I'll be right there."

Savannah nodded and followed the hostess.

Jillian turned back to Rose. "I wanted to ask how your sister was doing. I felt terrible about how frightened she was by Possum."

Rose's smile grew, turning her slightly plain face pretty. "I'd forgotten his name. That's so cute. My sister is fine. She was a little nervous for the rest of the day." Her smile slipped away. "Honestly, I worry about Lilly. She was always afraid of cats, but it got so much worse after her husband left." She sighed. "We've had a tough year as a family. It's why I left my job in Atlanta to come help out."

"I'm sorry," Jillian said. "Please, do tell Lilly that the flowers for the wedding were beautiful."

"I'm so glad," Rose said. "That was your first wedding at that venue, right? I think I remember hearing my sister say that."

"Yes, it was." Now it was Jillian's turn to sigh. "Unfortunately, the wedding didn't end up happening, but the flowers were beautiful, and I appreciate all the work you and your sister did on them."

Rose held up both hands. "It was all Lilly. My artistic skills are in makeup, not flower arranging."

"Is that what you did in Atlanta?" Jillian asked.

Rose nodded. "But I'm slowly learning about flowers, though Lilly definitely wouldn't leave me alone with an arrangement."

"Sounds like my grandmother and the bakery," Jillian said. "I guess we all have to learn in baby steps. I should go join my friend now. I don't want to interrupt your lunch too long. Please, send your sister my well-wishes."

Jillian looked around the room. The restaurant was certainly doing a booming business for the middle of the day. She spotted a hand waving from halfway across the room and saw that it was Savannah. With a smile on her face, she began heading in that direction. Along the way, she passed by the lighted salad bar where a lanky man with a fringe of gray hair and a questionable comb-over turned away from the salad offerings suddenly and nearly plowed right into Jillian.

"Watch yourself!" he demanded.

"Excuse me," Jillian said at exactly the same moment, then she frowned at his rude tone. "I think you're the one who wasn't watching."

"Leave it to you to blame someone else," he snapped. He took one hand from his plate so he could point a slightly gnarled finger at her. "I hope you learned from the fiasco of that wedding you planned. You need to stick to your own business. And remember, it's never a good idea to stab people in the back. You never know when the knife might find you next!"

With that, he stomped around Jillian, leaving her in the middle of the room with her mouth hanging open.

13

When Jillian reached the table, she slipped into her seat, feeling discombobulated from the unprovoked attack.

"What did Richard Meyer want?" Savannah asked.

"Richard Meyer?" Jillian said. "Was that the man's name? Apparently, he wanted to threaten me." She repeated what the man said.

Savannah winced. "I told you he was mad at you."

"You did?" Jillian tried to remember a conversation about strange balding men who held a grudge against her.

"Uh-huh, in this very room, though not this seat." Savannah waited a moment, then laughed. "Richard Meyer owns Dreams Come True."

"Oh," Jillian said. "I never met him before. Bertie handled all the contact during the one time we've worked with them since I came home. Now his bad temper makes more sense, though he was being overly dramatic."

"He can be that way," Savannah agreed. She pointed at the menu. "You might want to figure out what you want. I see the waitress coming."

Jillian snapped open the menu and put the grumpy wedding planner out of her head as she decided between a crab-cake Caesar salad and the "ultimate salad" that was topped with chicken and shrimp. She managed to choose before the waitress arrived, which she considered a good omen. Now if only she could keep the good luck going for the swamp trip in the morning.

The overcast skies on Tuesday morning made the long drive on narrow roads gloomy but easy on Jillian's eyes. She'd bathed for a ridiculously long time, reveling in it since she still had to avoid getting her bandaged head wet. Now she was allowed to leave the wound uncovered, so she French-braided her hair to hide the bald spot. At least she told herself that the braid hid it. So far, no one had been unkind enough to point out any bald scalp showing.

When Jillian pulled up at Savannah's house, her friend came out wearing khaki cargo shorts and a matching camp shirt, unbuttoned over a red tank. Hiking boots and long socks covered up most of the rest of the exposed skin on Savannah's legs. A khaki bucket hat was perched on her brown hair, completing the outfit. "Didn't the store have any pith helmets to go with your jungle-explorer costume?" Jillian asked as she stepped out of the car to better take in Savannah's fashion statement.

Savannah pointed at her. "Laugh now, but when you get swamp goo all over those linen shorts and end up having to throw away those expensive running shoes, you'll wish you were dressed this way."

Jillian had to admit her own clothing choices were less utilitarian, but her wardrobe wasn't exactly full of clothes designed to resist swamp slime. That had never been an issue in California. The closest she could come to explorer garb was a pair of neat linen shorts with button-tabbed cuffs and a roomy, pale-blue silky blouse that she hoped would breathe in the humid swamp air. "These shoes have very good treads," she said defensively. "Which should help if the ground is slippery."

Savannah held up the large tote bag she was carrying. "I also have bug repellent, sunscreen, and a first-aid kit. I tell you, you're going to be so glad you have me along."

"I'm already so glad I have you along," Jillian assured her. "I forgot to ask yesterday, but I hope this isn't tearing you away from any pressing work."

Savannah opened the passenger door and gave Jillian another grin before slipping inside. "You're totally tearing me way from my work. That's the best part."

The scenery on the drive to the swamp tended to be repetitious with lots of trees and farms and the occasional ranch home, some clearly manufactured and often surrounded by small outbuildings and scrubby lawns.

"I sometimes forget how rural Georgia is down in this area," Jillian said after passing another of an endless number of small farms. "I know Moss Hollow isn't exactly a steaming metropolis, but we do have multistory buildings."

"Moss Hollow has outlying farms too," Savannah said. "I've been out to goat farms, a couple of organic farms, and I even do the books for Vanguard Dairy, which is a big name for a place with exactly six cows."

"You know, I've never been close to a cow," Jillian said.

"They're nice, mostly," Savannah said. "Vanguard has Jerseys, so they're smallish cows, as cows go, with sweet faces. Peggy Vann let me try my hand at milking once. It was harder than it looks."

"How do tiny farms survive?" Jillian asked. "I see them at farmers' markets, but that doesn't seem enough for people to live on."

"You'd be surprised, though most also do community shares. You might look into that for the bakery, actually," Savannah said. "You could buy shares at some of the farms I know, and then they would provide all the milk, cheese, and eggs for the bakery. If you mentioned it in your advertising, it would help the farmers and you. People love to buy local."

Jillian nodded. "That's not a bad idea. I'll look into that as soon as we get this whole mess with the Blackwaters settled. I can tell you one thing I've decided: I'm never doing another wedding where there isn't a separate wedding planner."

"That's probably a good idea."

Her friend's voice sounded odd, and Jillian turned her head to look quickly at her. "Why do I think you know something I should hear?"

"Nothing really," Savannah said. "Just that Richard at Dreams Come True will be happy to know if this is your only foray into wedding planning."

Jillian harrumphed. "After the way he acted yesterday at Crazy Fish, I'm not overly concerned about his feelings."

"Richard has a temper, but he's not really a bad guy."

Jillian turned onto a narrow road, and the farms disappeared as trees started flanking both sides of the road.

Savannah picked up Jillian's smartphone from the console where it had been directing them through the trip. "We're almost there, I think."

"I'll be glad for that," Jillian said. "I'm ready to get out and stretch my legs, even if it is in swampland."

Savannah glanced up from the phone and quickly pointed. "There's the sign." A wooden sign with what looked like a flying goose on it marked the entrance to the Okefenokee National Wildlife Refuge. Jillian turned up the narrow road into the park. The trees on either side of the road were tall but almost spindly thin, with lots of thick underbrush at the base. "I thought everything would look wetter," Jillian said. "Swamps in movies have lots of drippy moss and dark shadows. This is actually pretty."

"There are a lot of pretty spots in the swamp," Savannah said. "You really shouldn't count on movies for accurate representations of wild places."

"I don't just count on movies," Jillian said. "I watch nature documentaries too."

They skirted a couple of loops marked by informational signs and access markers for walking trails. Jillian didn't slow enough to see them closely.

They also passed some isolated buildings before coming to the open gates where signs announced there was a pay station ahead for their entrance fee to the park. Another sign let them know that visiting hours began a half hour before sunrise and ended at seven thirty in the evening. "I certainly hope we're done here well before then," Jillian said.

"If we're here after the sun sets, I'm not sure any amount of bug spray will keep us from being bled dry by mosquitoes."

Jillian thought that was a cheery image but simply drove on. They finally reached a line of cones, detouring them slightly off the road to a tiny fee booth that looked more like a child's playhouse than any kind of official structure. They paid for a daily permit and drove on to the visitor's center, featuring several buildings with pale walls and green metal roofs.

The park rangers Jillian spotted at the center all wore dark-green shorts with matching baseball caps and pale-khaki polo shirts. Both the shirts and the hats bore the park insignia. They loaded her up with maps and information for finding Duvall Island.

"You can drive there from here," a freckle-faced female ranger said. "Some of the islands actually have to be reached by boat, but Duvall is part of our main information area, so there is a footbridge. The homestead is well maintained. If you come back for our open house in October, we have demonstrations of soapmaking and four-note singing performances."

"If we have a good time today, maybe we'll come back," Jillian said, though she sincerely doubted she was telling the truth. She couldn't imagine having a good enough day that she'd make a visit to the swamp for fun. She reached into her purse and pulled

out a picture she'd printed that morning. It was a copy of the torn
photo she'd found in Gordon's house. "Could you tell me if you
recognize either of these men?"

The ranger held the print close to her nose. "I don't know
this guy," she said pointing, "but I think the other one is Jacob."

"You know Jacob Zimmer?"

"Was that his last name?" The young ranger smiled. "I only
knew his name was Jacob. He used to come out a lot to see the
Duvall homestead. He hasn't been around in a while."

"That's because he disappeared, here in the swamp." Jillian
looked at her doubtfully. "I would think you'd know that."

The young ranger shook her head. "The times I remember
him coming here were before I had my baby. I guess he could have
disappeared while I was on maternity leave." Her smile dropped.
"Sometimes people do go missing in the swamp. I didn't know
Jacob was one of them. He was always nice."

"Is there anyone here who could tell me more about him?"
Jillian asked.

"Not that I know of, but you might ask out at the homestead."

After a quick rest stop and a snack, they piled back into
Jillian's car and followed the ranger's directions to the Duvall
Island homestead.

Jillian spotted a sign and pulled into a small, well-cared-for
parking lot. The walking trail to the homestead was wide and
level. "Clearly my shoes aren't going to be as much of an issue as
you thought," Jillian said as she swung open her door.

"We'll see."

Though the morning had been almost cool when she left Belle
Haven, it was a thick, sticky hot on the trail to the house. Jillian
waved a hand at the whine of an insect in her ear, and Savannah
passed her a bottle of insect repellent from her tote bag. All around
them the woods were full of sounds—hums and whines and faint

crashing in the brush. "Don't people talk about how peaceful and quiet the woods are?"

"These aren't woods," Savannah said. "They're swamps. They're never quiet."

They soon spotted a ragged fence and some worn wooden buildings with metal roofs beyond. The big trees around the clearing were more what Jillian had expected from a swamp: gnarled and full of hanging strands of moss. "That must be the homestead," Jillian said. "We need to find someone who might have seen Gordon or Jacob."

The search didn't take long. They spotted a young woman coming out of one of the buildings, carrying a bucket. Her honey-brown hair was pulled back into a ponytail that swung as she practically hopped down the worn wooden steps, her face as sunny as her walk was sprightly.

"Excuse me?" Jillian said as she angled to intercept the woman. "Do you work here?"

"I volunteer here," the woman said, pointing with her free hand at a badge on her chest that identified her as Emmy Duvall, volunteer. "This was my family's land when they were swampers, a long time ago."

"It's an interesting place," Jillian said as she fumbled on her phone for the photo she had shown the young ranger earlier. She pulled it out of her bag and held it up. "Do you know either of these men?"

Emmy leaned close, then nodded. "Of course. That's Jacob and his friend. Gordon, I think his name was. Jacob was the feller who disappeared out here."

With a rush of excitement at her success, Jillian exchanged looks with Savannah. "Did you know Jacob well?"

"Not really. He came out here a lot. He was nice and loved hearing stories about my family, but he didn't talk about himself much. He asked questions, mostly about the old stories and the haints."

"The haints?" Jillian asked.

"On the island." The girl's voice was so matter of fact that she reminded Jillian of her great-aunt, assuming that ghosts were a normal part of any conversation.

"Do you believe there are ghosts on the island?"

"Of course. I've seen them in the evening when the shadows grow long. And I've heard them in the buildings, walking and whispering. It's kind of nice, since I know they're all family."

Aunt Cornelia would love you, Jillian thought. "And you saw Gordon out here too?" Jillian tapped the photo again.

"A couple of times. When he came with Jacob, they didn't stop and chat. I only know the guy's name was Gordon because I overheard them talking." Her expression turned alarmed. "Not that I eavesdropped. It's just that sometimes we were in the same buildings at the same time."

"I'm sure you didn't do anything wrong," Jillian said. "But you did hear them talking. Was it about ghosts?"

The young woman shook her head. "Not usually. I think Jacob brought his friend out here when he was having girlfriend trouble. They usually talked about some girl named Alice. Apparently she was a handful." The young woman's cheeks pinked slightly. "Oh dear, pretend I didn't say that. Y'all are way too easy to talk to, and I'm shooting off my mouth. I should get back to work."

Jillian spoke quickly to head off the girl before she could leave. "Do you know what happened to Jacob?"

The girl's cheery face grew somber, just as the young ranger's had. "Not really. I saw him on the day he disappeared. He walked right by me without saying anything, which wasn't like Jacob at all. I thought he might be coming down with a cold or something, though. He looked kind of peaked."

"Peaked how?" Jillian asked.

The girl set the bucket down and shoved her hands in the pockets of her khaki pants. "I dunno exactly. I remember thinking he didn't look so good, but I'm not sure exactly how." She sighed. "Now I wish I'd stopped him and talked a while. Maybe he wouldn't have gone wherever he went and disappeared."

"Did you see which way he was going?"

The girl shrugged. "If I had to guess, I'd say he went out to the bird-watching tower, or at least out on the boardwalk. He often went out to the tower and stared over the swamp for hours. You can see a long ways from the top of the tower."

"Which way is that?" Jillian asked. "Can we go out there?"

The girl shook her head. "No, sorry. We had a fire about a year ago, and it burned up a big piece of the boardwalk and took down the tower. It's taken the park forever to get the funding to rebuild, so they've just barely started. You can only walk out to a couple dozen feet past the first covered shelter."

"About a year ago." Savannah stepped closer to speak. "How long after Jacob's disappearance was that?"

"The fire started that very night," Emmy said. "It was a thunderstorm that eventually drove the searchers out of the swamp. Then right in the middle of the storm, lightning struck the boardwalk and started the fire. People think that you don't have to be careful with fire because this is wetlands, but the wood here is *old*. It was a miracle the firefighters were able to put it out before it reached the homestead. Can you imagine how fast these buildings would go up? And we'd lose all this history." She looked off into the distance, her face still sad; then she seemed to shake off the mood and looked at Jillian with her cheery expression again. "Anyway, if y'all come back for our October open house, the boardwalk and tower will be back up and better than ever. They're making it out of some kind of fireproof composite material instead of wood, so I hear."

"Other than the tower," Savannah said, "did Jacob have any other favorite spots here on the island?"

Emmy shook her head. "Not really. He used to go in the house sometimes. He said he enjoyed listening to the haints." She pointed toward the building they'd seen her exit.

"Then I guess that's our next stop," Jillian said. "Thank you for talking with us. Are you going to be around for a while, in case I think of any other questions?"

"Sure will." She waved at them and headed off toward one of the smaller buildings with the bucket.

Jillian and Savannah walked side by side to the steps leading up to the front porch of the house. The wood of the steps, the porch, and the house itself wore the splotchy colors of age and humidity, pale gray in some places and nearly red in others. A brick chimney ran up the side of the house, so Jillian wasn't surprised to spot a fireplace as they walked into the cozy interior. The walls were all wood clad, and the furniture was simple, though not as rough as Jillian had expected.

The floors groaned under their feet, and the air had the sharp smell of age with a hint of woodsmoke mixed in. "It's no wonder people imagine ghosts in here," Savannah said. She walked over to rest her hand on the hand pump that had provided the water for the kitchen sink. "Makes me really appreciate the magic of modern conveniences."

Jillian stood still a moment, looking around the room and listening. "This is an interesting old building, but I can't imagine what would bring Jacob out here again and again. Even as a ghost hunter, he wouldn't need to visit more than once or twice."

Savannah shrugged. "I don't know how ghost hunting works."

"Neither do I." *But maybe I need to find out.* "I don't think we're going to learn anything new in these buildings."

"What's next?" Savannah asked. "Do we go home?"

Jillian shoved her hands into her pants pockets and rocked on her toes as she thought. "Yeah, but let's walk out on the boardwalk as far as we can first. I don't expect we'll find anything there either, but maybe we'll get some insight into whatever drove Jacob to come here."

"Maybe we'll run into a ghost who can answer questions," Savannah said brightly.

"I know we're operating blind here, but I need to feel that I tried. Alice will be looking for updates, and I'll need something to tell her."

"I understand." Savannah waved her hand toward the door. "Lead on. I wouldn't mind seeing the boardwalk."

They ambled down the trail to the boardwalk, neither one of them talking for the few minutes it took. The swamp rose up around them, buzzing with life and dripping with humidity. Jillian couldn't imagine how horrible it must be in the middle of summer. "Can you imagine making your life out here?"

"I think the swampers were a tough bunch, and independent."

"Sounds like my grandmother."

Savannah laughed. "I bet Bertie would have made an excellent swamper. I can't imagine her letting the government take her land to make a national park."

"I imagine that wasn't an easy transition for a lot of the swampers. The independence and distrust of government that brought them out here wouldn't have made it easy to give up their land."

They reached the beginning of the boardwalk. The transition from paved trail to boardwalk was smooth as the boardwalk was raised only inches from the surface of the ground beneath. Everywhere around them, the swamp was green and brown, almost alarmingly full of life.

"Oh, Jillian, look." Savannah walked to the edge of the board-walk and knelt, pointing. "Pitcher plants. I remember when we learned about those in elementary school. The plants that eat insects. I had dreams about sliding down the throat of a pitcher plant for weeks."

Jillian vaguely remembered the lesson Savannah described, though she'd not found it alarming. She had been too practical, even as a child, knowing that a plant that ate flies would hardly be able to gobble down children. She squatted beside Savannah and looked over the long tubular plants with their brown hoods. They certainly didn't look like the stuff of childhood nightmares.

"If Jacob came out here to be alone, I could understand it," Jillian said as she stood back up and dusted off the hand she'd used to steady herself on the boardwalk. "Even though we're not far from other people, it feels so lonely out here." She started continuing down the boardwalk, and Savannah followed her. "His visits would make sense if he was a botanist or any kind of biologist, but a ghost hunter? We're missing something important here."

"You know, it is secluded out here," Savannah said. "Even in the summer, I bet it isn't too hard to find spots to be alone. Maybe he was meeting someone out here."

"Meeting someone?" Jillian said. "You think he was cheating on Alice?"

Savannah shrugged. "Actually, I was thinking it would be a good spot to conduct all kinds of illicit activities."

"Drugs, maybe," Jillian said. "But, honestly, there are plenty of such spots near Moss Hollow too."

"True, but maybe this was a halfway point. If he was meeting someone from Florida, say, this might be a good spot. And I believe Florida has a thriving drug trade."

"A drug deal gone bad could certainly cause someone to disappear," Jillian agreed.

They strolled on. Jillian was determined to walk as far as

they were able, though she couldn't really say why. Frustration probably. She had no other real leads, so she'd follow this one until she had to stop.

Up ahead they saw a small offshoot from the boardwalk, a covered shelter with a built-in bench and sturdy wooden rails. Savannah stopped to read a sign at the shelter. "This shelter was built over an alligator hole."

"I wonder how the alligator felt about that," Jillian said. She walked to the rail and looked out into the swamp. There was no confusing the area with a normal stand of woods anymore. The ground, what ground they could see, looked soft with plenty of standing water surrounding every thin, moss-covered tree.

With her hands resting on the rail, Jillian leaned forward, peering into the shadows at something that didn't belong. She was so caught up in trying to discern what she was seeing that she didn't notice the anole lizard sunning on the railing. He took that moment to race across the wood, up and over Jillian's hand. She shrieked at the contact, jumping back.

Savannah laughed. "I don't think the anole would hurt you."

"I didn't see it until after I screamed," Jillian said sheepishly. "Honestly, I thought it might be a snake or a spider." She shuddered as she rubbed her hand. "I'm losing my appreciation for the swamp just thinking about it."

"What were you looking at anyway?" Savannah asked as she looked out over the swamp.

"Something over by that thicker tree." Jillian pointed. "Can you see? Something is catching the light. It doesn't look natural."

Savannah leaned forward over the rail. "It's hard to see in the shadows over there." Her face brightened. "Wait, I have just the thing." She rooted through her oversize purse and pulled out a sturdy flashlight. "This thing is supposed to be strong enough to guide aircraft."

Savannah turned on the flashlight, and both women peered toward the tree as the light chased away the shadows. Jillian gasped. "That's a top hat. More than that, it's Gordon's top hat."

"That's kind of a leap," Savannah said. "I know it's a huge coincidence to find a top hat right after a guy disappears who was on the way to a wedding, but it could be left over from a different wedding. They sometimes have weddings here. Some people *love* swamps."

"Gordon's hat was unique," Jillian said. "Alice sewed a bunch of *Alice in Wonderland* charms on the hatband. It's those bits of metal that are catching the light. That's Gordon's hat, and I'm going to go get it."

Savannah's eyes widened. "You're going to wade out in the swamp? There's no way to tell how deep that water is. Plus, aren't swamps full of quicksand?"

"You have an amazingly vivid imagination," Jillian said as she stepped up on the bench to boost herself over the railing. "Wait here, and I'll get the hat."

"You're going to ruin those shorts," Savannah said. "I should go."

"I have other shorts," Jillian said as she carefully eased herself down into the murky water. "It's worth it for the cause. If that is Gordon's hat, we'll know both of Alice's fiancés vanished out here."

"A disturbing thought," Savannah agreed. "Jillian, you do remember that this stand was built over an alligator nest?"

"Do you see any alligators? Me neither. It must be off doing alligator things. Or it moved away when they decided to build a boardwalk over its house. Besides, I'm only going to be in the water for a minute." She let go of the boardwalk and slopped along in the shin-deep water. It soaked through her shoes and socks, making her shudder from the quick chill. The water was choked with weeds, making it thick and difficult to push through.

Plus, mud under the water sucked at Jillian's shoes, requiring effort to pull free with each step. She waded awkwardly over to the tree, grateful that it wasn't any farther away.

When she finally reached her destination, she leaned against the tree for a moment, panting from the effort. She was out of shape since she'd given up the daily trips to the gym that had been part of her life in California. Of course, she made more money then and could afford things like gym memberships. Plus, in California, she hadn't worked a job that began as the sun was peeking over the horizon.

Jillian snatched up the hat and turned it over and over in her hands. She examined the collection of watch-faced charms that Alice had stitched to the wide black hatband. "This is definitely Gordon's hat," she called. She looked out over the swamp. *Is Gordon here somewhere?*

She turned to wave the hat at Savannah. To her surprise, her friend's eyes were wide in horror as she pointed at the water not far from where Jillian stood. A rough sunken log broke free from the shadows near another large tree and began moving toward her. As the light hit it, it became clear it was no log.

It was an alligator, and it was heading right for Jillian.

"Run!" Savannah screamed.

14

Jillian shoved the muddy hat on her head and began wading back toward the boardwalk, horrified by her sluggish speed. The alligator was a natural in the water and would certainly reach her long before she reached the boardwalk.

"Hurry!" Savannah yelled.

"I *am* hurrying!" Jillian yelled back, though she knew she wasn't. She was thrashing and wallowing like a perfect alligator snack.

Something suddenly flew through the air by Jillian, who turned to see what it was. The heavy flashlight struck the alligator above one eye, making the creature thrash in the water and giving Jillian some valuable extra time. But would it be enough?

"Run!" Savannah bellowed again, and Jillian wallowed her way to the edge of the shelter as quickly as she could. The thrashing behind her ended, and she assumed that meant the alligator was after her again, but she didn't turn around. She had often yelled at the television when the heroine wasted valuable time looking behind her. Now she knew exactly how strong the urge was.

She reached out and snagged one of the posts of the shelter, hauling herself out of the muck. She swung around the edge of the shelter and stumbled toward Savannah. "You don't think the alligator will come up here, do you?"

"I don't think alligators are as fast on land," Savannah said. "But I would prefer we didn't hang around to find out."

Jillian agreed. They needed to get back and alert the authorities to the discovery of Gordon's hat. They ran along the boardwalk, and both women kept a sharp eye out for any movement in the swamp, but no more alligators materialized.

As it turned out, the authorities weren't overly impressed by Gordon's hat, even when Jillian insisted it was one of a kind and definitely belonged to the missing man. No one had seen Gordon come into the swamp, though they admitted it was a busy weekend with lots of visitors enjoying the last of the cooler weather before the coming summer. Without more to go on, as when Jacob had disappeared, the park rangers weren't going to launch an expensive and exhaustive manhunt.

When Jillian got home, she luxuriated in a hot bath until her fingers and toes turned to prunes, trying to soak away the feeling and smell of the swamp. When she felt human again, she pulled on yoga pants and a T-shirt, and headed down to her office to do more computer research, this time to see what she could find about the Lowlands Paranormal Investigators.

The shadows in the office felt unusually creepy after the events of the last few days. Jillian pulled back the curtains, letting in the late-afternoon light. She could practically hear her grandmother nagging her about light fading the furniture. "It's okay," Jillian muttered. "This stuff is all prefaded for my convenience."

The website for the Lowlands Paranormal Investigators had black backgrounds, sickly green text, and blurry photographs. They listed their membership at eight investigators and included a strange but touching tribute to Jacob.

With her chin resting in the palm of her hand, Jillian winced frequently as she read through the tribute, written in bad rhyming verse. The spooky background music that insisted on playing when she opened the page didn't help, and the ornate font made reading difficult.

She jumped when her office door creaked open ominously, going well with the creepy music. Her great-aunt walked in, carrying a tray. Possum trotted along behind her.

"I brought you some tea and cookies," Aunt Cornelia said as she settled the tray on the desk. She gave Jillian a sympathetic look. "I saw your nice shorts. I don't think you're going to get those stains out of linen."

"Probably not. I'll take them to the cleaners tomorrow."

Aunt Cornelia peered at the computer screen, then her face lit up. "The Lowlands Paranormal Investigators! Are you finally becoming interested in the paranormal? I've been wanting to attend one of their meetings, but those groups are usually so full of young people, I wasn't sure I'd fit in."

"You've heard of them?"

"Of course! They're doing a program at the Moss Hollow Library tomorrow night. I twisted Josi Rosenschein's arm to get her to invite them. I thought I'd be going all by myself, but if you're interested . . ."

Jillian wondered if there was an easy way to talk her great-aunt out of an interest in the group, but none came to mind, and she had more pressing concerns. "What time is the presentation?"

Cornelia clapped her hands. "Does that mean you're going to come with me? It's at seven, but we should probably go early so we can get good seats."

Jillian imagined that wouldn't be a problem, but she was beginning to think the people of Moss Hollow would always surprise her. She promised Cornelia they'd get an early start, then turned her attention to writing an e-mail to Alice. She didn't have much to offer that was encouraging, but she felt Alice deserved the truth.

The Moss Hollow Library was small but inviting. Jillian almost always felt a warm glow when she walked on the hardwood floors and watched groups quietly discussing books in the comfy chairs near the front window, but that night, all she felt was a mixture of embarrassment and apprehension. In all honesty, she hated the idea of being seen at a slide show about the paranormal.

The library only had one meeting room. Its capacity topped out around fifty people. Thankfully, as Jillian had predicted, that wasn't a problem, though Josi had optimistically set out at least thirty chairs in neat rows facing a podium and portable screen. The man standing behind the podium had a young face and thinning red hair. Jillian guessed he was in his late twenties or early thirties. He wore jeans and a T-shirt with bright-green lettering: *LPI*. He studied the screen on his laptop intently through thick eyeglasses. In the front row, a slightly chubby young woman with long, coal-black hair seemed to be calling out directions for whatever he was doing. Something about the young woman struck Jillian as familiar, but she couldn't place her.

"I knew we should have come earlier," Cornelia said fretfully. "The whole front row is full."

"That's too bad," Jillian said. She hated to disappoint her great-aunt, but she had no intention of sitting at the front of the room. She wanted to watch the people, not the show. Her gaze swept over those already seated, and she blinked in surprise. Rose, the sister of Lilly Quest, sat perched nervously on the edge of a chair on an aisle seat about halfway down. As with many of the chairs in the room, the two chairs next to Rose were empty. "I see a spot," Jillian said, heading right for Rose.

Cornelia followed behind her, fretfully. "Are you sure? I thought we might sit closer up."

"And I thought we'd sit in the last row," Jillian responded. "Let's consider this a compromise."

"Oh, all right." Cornelia's mouth closed in a thin line that made her look more like her twin sister than usual. "But I should say hello to Destiny first."

"Destiny?" Jillian repeated.

Aunt Cornelia waved vaguely toward the front, being entirely too well-raised and Southern to simply point, so Jillian knew who she meant. "I met her at the hospital when I was waiting for you to be patched up. That's how I knew about this group and why I asked Josi to get them to visit us here. We were lucky they were able to come right away."

"Lucky," Jillian echoed, then she realized who her great-aunt had meant. The young woman with the long dark hair *had* been in the hospital waiting room, dressed as a carnival fortune-teller. Jillian hadn't recognized her in relatively normal clothes of black leggings, a long glossy black shirt, and a black leather vest. "She does seem to enjoy black."

"It's soothing for the spirits," Cornelia said. "She told me. Which probably explains why I haven't been very successful contacting the Belle Haven haint. I don't own black clothes other than a couple of dresses that I normally reserve for funerals." She looked pointedly toward Destiny. "I wonder how I would look in an outfit like that."

Ridiculous, Jillian thought, but she decided on a more diplomatic reply. "I don't think it's your style."

Aunt Cornelia nodded. "I do prefer florals. Maybe I could get a dress with black flowers."

Jillian shuddered slightly at the ghastly image.

They'd reached the aisle where Rose sat so Jillian put on a

smile. "Rose, how nice to see you. Are those seats taken?"

Rose looked up at her in surprise and stammered as she stood to let them into the aisle. "N-no, I'm here alone. Um, it's nice to see you, Miss Green."

"Please, call me Jillian. And this is my aunt, Cornelia." She slipped by the florist and took the seat directly beside her. As Rose sank back down onto the metal folding chair, Jillian watched her carefully. "Are you interested in the paranormal?"

"Not really," Rose said faintly, then cleared her throat and spoke with more force. "I thought it would be something different. I guess I'm a bit adrift. In Atlanta, there were always so many choices for things to do."

Cornelia leaned over Jillian to speak to Rose. "Our house is haunted."

"No, it's not," Jillian said.

Cornelia behaved as if Jillian hadn't spoken. "It has been for generations. The Belle Haven haint is practically famous. I'm thinking of having the Paranormal Investigators come out to see if they can make contact."

Jillian looked at her great-aunt in horror. "No."

Cornelia tutted at her as if Jillian had said something silly. "I haven't been terribly successful at contacting the poor ghost. Getting professionals out to see what's going on seems sensible to me, especially since our haint has been attracting new ghosts to the estate."

Jillian gawked at her. "What are you talking about?"

"The angry ghost of that poor young man, of course." Again, her great-aunt turned her attention to Rose. "We had a visitation the other night at a wedding rehearsal. I, of course, had felt his angry presence earlier. I'm quite sensitive, but I haven't been able to make contact with him since."

"You've been trying to make contact with a prank ghost?" Jillian asked. "How have you done that?"

"The usual way," Cornelia said. "Raymond and I have been walking around the area of the manifestation, calling out to the ghost. He hasn't returned. I wonder if he'd come back if Alice came over."

Jillian waved her hand. "You may not contact our client about this." She pointed at Cornelia. "I'll tell Bertie."

Jillian realized she'd been hearing quiet snorting sounds from Rose for several moments as the young woman tried to repress laughter. Apparently, she'd given up holding it back and broke into giggles.

"I'm so glad I came to this," Rose said. "No matter what the presentation turns out to be, you two are worth the price of admission."

Jillian felt warmth climb into her cheeks. She tried not to get into wacky conversations with Cornelia in public. She looked around and realized from the smiles of those seated nearby that Rose wasn't the only one enjoying their discussion. She leaned closer to Cornelia and whispered, "We will discuss this later."

Her great-aunt sniffed dismissively and turned away to focus on the front of the room with her hands folded primly over the purse in her lap. The man behind the podium had stopped fiddling with his laptop and was looking out over the audience, his face a mask of panic.

About half of the seats in the room were filled, and Jillian glanced down at her watch. It was time to begin, though punctuality was a liquid thing in the South.

"Hello?" The speaker behind the podium shifted from foot to foot, his attention flickering between the dark-haired young woman and his computer screen. "I mean, good evening. Thank you for coming out to hear about our investigations. I'm from the Lowlands Paranormal Investigators." He paused, and his gaze skimmed the audience quickly.

Cornelia sat up straighter and clapped her hands. No one else in the audience joined her, but the speaker's cheeks reddened. A quick smile darted across his face, and he nodded at Cornelia before pushing his glasses up on his nose and continuing. His presentation turned out to be more than a little confusing. The liberal sprinkling of odd jargon and acronyms didn't mean much to Jillian. *EVP? EMF?*

The photos that flashed on the screen behind the young man were mostly blurry shadows or grainy shots with odd light spots. Jillian had to fight the urge to laugh aloud at one or two of the photos where the proof of ghostly activity seemed particularly nebulous. She glanced sideways at Cornelia, whose face showed rapt fascination, occasionally jotting notes on a pad she'd pulled from her purse.

When the presentation wrapped up, Cornelia popped up like a kid's toy and pulled on Jillian's arm. "Come along. I want to speak with that young man."

"So do I," Jillian said, though she was certain her topic of conversation would be far different from Cornelia's.

They slipped by Rose, and Jillian bid her a hasty good-bye. The budding florist grinned and waved.

As they walked to the front, the young woman with the long black hair called out to Cornelia. "I remember you from the hospital! You live in a haunted mansion, right?"

"You are Destiny, right?" Cornelia's cheeks pinked in a flattered fluster. "You remembered? I'm sure you hear about so many."

"Quite a few," the woman said, "but we're always interested in the older homes. Didn't you say yours was an old plantation house?"

Again, Cornelia looked pleased. "That's right."

"We'd love to come out to do an investigation," Destiny said, turning to look at the man. "Wouldn't we, Russ?"

He blinked at her several times. "What?"

"This is the lady from the plantation. I told you about her on the drive over. I'm going to tell the group at the next meeting."

He looked at Cornelia a bit vaguely. "Right." He shifted from foot to foot for a moment, then bobbed his head. "Nice to meet you."

Jillian stepped carefully around Cornelia and thrust out her hand at the man. "It's nice to meet you too. I'm Jillian Green. This is my aunt, Cornelia Montgomery. I understand Jacob Zimmer was in your group?"

The unexpected introduction of Jacob's name seemed to leave the man speechless. He stared at her for a moment with a hand partly raised for shaking.

Jillian reached out and pumped his cold hand a few times. "And you are Russ?"

Waking from his confused stupor, he nodded. "Russel Luman."

Destiny popped up from the seat and squeezed in between Jillian and Russel. "You knew Jacob?"

"I know his former fiancée better," Jillian said. "Alice Blackwater."

"I never met her. She wasn't a believer."

"She is now," Cornelia interjected, and Jillian frowned at her great-aunt. "Jacob showed up at her wedding rehearsal dinner."

The woman's eyes widened. "There was a manifestation? What made you think it was Jacob?"

"Alice recognized him," Cornelia said. "And he called her name."

The woman turned to exchange looks with the man, who still looked a little bewildered. "A visual and auditory manifestation! I don't suppose anyone caught it on tape?"

"Mostly we were focused on Alice since she fainted," Jillian said dryly. "Actually, as long as we're talking about Jacob, I have a specific question to ask. Do you know why he was so obsessed with the Okefenokee Swamp, and Duvall Island in particular?"

The woman's bright expression darkened. "No, I never understood it. I mean, yeah, there are tons of stories of manifestations in the swamp. Plus, there are the giant skeletons found on Duvall Island. But Jacob went out there all the time. And he never wanted us to come. What kind of investigation is that?"

Russ cleared his throat. "Destiny, you know Jacob enjoyed working solo. He was always that way." He turned and gave Jillian a nervous smile. "A lot of us aren't really socially adept."

"So Jacob was uncomfortable around people?" Jillian asked. She'd not heard anything about Jacob having social anxiety.

"Not the same as Russ," Destiny said. "But Jacob barely came to meetings. If it wasn't for Duvall Island, I'm not sure he would have been interested in the paranormal at all."

"Was there anyone in the group who was close to Jacob?" Jillian asked.

Destiny shook her head. "I probably knew him as well as anyone, and that wasn't that well. Most of our members are kind of . . . well, shy, I guess. So they don't push. Me, I push."

"But pushing didn't help?" Jillian asked.

"It wouldn't get him to tell me anything about what he was studying." Destiny wrapped her arms around herself. "Not that I wanted to be invited along on some investigation in the swamp. Still, most of us *enjoy* talking about our investigations."

"But Jacob didn't."

She shook her head. "He wasn't rude about it, but every bit of information was like pulling teeth. I thought he'd eventually come back to the group with something big. I mean, he was out there all the time. And he started opening his shop less and less. Something had to be up."

"So his swamp investigation was affecting his work at the antique shop?" Jillian asked.

Destiny nodded. "I dropped by the shop a couple times, thinking maybe he'd talk more away from the meetings, you know? But the place was always closed."

"This is all very interesting," Cornelia interjected, "but I was hoping to talk about an investigation at Belle Haven. I've been trying to make contact ever since the passing of my dear husband, Raymond."

Destiny looked confused for a moment. "You're trying to make contact with your husband?"

Cornelia waved a hand. "No, of course not. I see Raymond all the time. I'm trying to make contact with the Belle Haven haint, the ghost of Virginia Belle. She was the wife of my ancestor, Captain Hoyt Belle. I've sensed her presence several times and had some minor encounters, but she is elusive."

"So your house is haunted by Virginia Belle and your late husband?" Destiny asked.

Cornelia laughed. "Of course not. Raymond would never resort to haunting. He was far too dignified. No, he has simply returned."

Destiny spoke slowly, as if lingering on each word would somehow make the content sensible. "Your husband has returned from the dead, but not as a ghost."

Cornelia smiled at her proudly, like a teacher whose student is finally breaking a tough equation. "Right."

Jillian reached up to rub at the pain beginning to form between her eyes as she wondered if there was any way to stop Cornelia from continuing her explanation. "I'm sure they aren't interested . . ."

"We're very interested," Destiny insisted. "How has he returned?"

"Raymond uses our cat," Cornelia said.

"Your husband speaks through your cat," Destiny said, again drawing the words out slowly.

"Technically, Possum is my sister's cat, but it's clear that he's housing my husband's spirit. He is quite devoted to me since I moved back to the house."

"Because you constantly sneak him treats," Jillian said.

Cornelia gave her a pitying look. "My niece is so closed off. My sister is the same way."

"Which means Bertie definitely doesn't want any ghost hunters traipsing around the property," Jillian warned.

Cornelia glared at Jillian for a moment but then gave up and sighed. "My niece is quite correct. My sister would never allow an investigation, though I do think one would be helpful, especially in light of the ghostly manifestation of Jacob Zimmer."

"You saw the ghost of Jacob Zimmer?"

Jillian nearly groaned aloud at the new voice joining the conversation. She turned to see who was speaking and was surprised to find Rose standing in the aisle behind her. Jillian raised her eyebrows. "You knew Jacob Zimmer?"

"I should hope so," Rose said. "He was my brother. My twin brother."

15

Jillian gawked at the young woman behind her.

The young woman returned the look with a slight smile. "I'm Rose Zimmer. I didn't know you knew my brother."

"I didn't," Jillian said. "I know his ex-fiancée."

Rose nodded. "Yes, Lilly told me the flowers were for Alice Blackwater's wedding. I honestly couldn't believe Lilly accepted the job, but I don't suppose any business can afford to turn down work these days." She wrinkled her nose in distaste. "Apparently, Alice got over the loss of my brother well enough."

"It *has* been a year," Jillian said. She noticed the intent interest of both her great-aunt and the paranormal investigators and cleared her throat. "Perhaps we shouldn't talk about this here." She wondered how to get the young woman alone to ask her some questions.

"I don't see why not," Rose said. "We are talking about my brother's ghost. Where did you see it?"

"I didn't see a ghost."

"At the estate," Cornelia said. "Your brother appeared in the back garden."

Jillian held up her hand. "I'm sorry, but someone showed up in our back garden in a rather horrific ghost costume as a rude prank against Alice Blackwater and Gordon Liddell. It was a flesh-and-blood person who left footprints and sludge from his costume."

Destiny clapped her hands together behind Jillian. "Footprints? Sludge? You found physical manifestations of the haunting." She turned to Russ. "Physical evidence! We *must* investigate this."

Russ cleared his throat and shoved his glasses up on his nose again. "It does sound promising."

"No, it doesn't," Jillian snapped. Then she made an effort to speak more calmly. "It was a prank, not a ghost." She turned to Rose. "I'm sorry. It was a horribly insensitive prank, and we do not know who was behind it, but it was not a ghost."

Rose nodded slowly. "Of course not." Her eyes began to shine, and she blinked several times before adding in a slightly husky voice, "Still, if my brother *were* trying to communicate . . ."

"I'm sorry about your brother, truly," Jillian said. "But he isn't haunting Belle Haven. Nothing is haunting Belle Haven. We won't be having any kind of paranormal investigation. End of story."

Rose started to speak, then closed her mouth, pressing her lips together in an unhappy line. Jillian felt badly about upsetting the young woman, but she wasn't having ghost hunters poking around Belle Haven. She was willing to humor her great-aunt and her craziness, but she wasn't going that far.

Naturally, that wasn't the end of the story. When they got home, Cornelia began to badger Bertie immediately. Bertie blamed Jillian for the annoyance since Jillian had gone with her to see the "whackadoodle ghost hunters."

"I don't know why you're blaming me," Jillian complained the next morning at the breakfast table. "I said no right there at the meeting."

Bertie grumbled something, but Jillian didn't catch it and decided she didn't really want to know. She saw the newspaper lying at one corner of the table and picked it up, risking another scolding since neither her great-aunt nor her grandmother believed in reading the paper at the table. They felt it was the low-tech equivalent of texting while sharing a meal.

Opening the paper, Jillian's eye went right for a small article at the bottom of the front page: *Local Celebrity Left at the Altar—Again!* Jillian groaned as she skimmed the piece and saw Belle Haven mentioned as the venue for the wedding.

"What now?" Bertie demanded.

"We made the papers," Jillian said quietly. "Or the house did. It's an article about Gordon's disappearance and mentions Belle Haven as the location for the wedding."

Bertie narrowed her eyes. "It doesn't say anything bad about the house, does it?"

"No, it's not a review. It's an article about Alice having had two fiancés vanish."

"That is odd," Cornelia said. "You shouldn't be reading the paper. It's bad for your digestion. Here, dear." She shoved a plate of biscuits toward Jillian, who gave in and set the paper aside.

She picked up one of Cornelia's perfect Southern biscuits, an indulgence that suggested Cornelia was trying to win over Bertie with food to get permission for the ghost hunting. Jillian felt slightly guilty for being so glad Cornelia couldn't possibly win this fight, but that didn't mean Jillian couldn't enjoy the fluffy biscuit perfection with a little butter and honey.

She bit into the warm biscuit and chewed quietly, thinking about the short article. At least the newspaper hadn't mentioned either the ghost or the crazy coincidence of the florists for Alice's wedding being relatives of the girl's first fiancé. The more she thought about the florist, the weirder it got. Jillian hadn't chosen Quest for Flowers from the phone book, nor were they on the original list of required vendors. Jillian had received their business card and a note from Mrs. Blackwater in the mail one day early on in the planning.

Did Alice's mother know she was hiring Jacob's sisters? Did she do it for some specific reason?

The questions continued to swirl in Jillian's head all morning as she filled éclairs and frosted bunny cupcakes. Bertie had added hot cross buns to the regular baking schedule until Easter, and the yeasty smell of the sweet buns filled the kitchen and drifted into the dining and pickup area and beyond into the street, pulling customers right off the sidewalks and into the shop all day.

"You look like your brain is stewing," Lenora said as she picked up a tray of filled éclairs. "What are you thinking about?"

"Alice Blackwater's wedding," Jillian said as she put a sheet of parchment into a new empty pan. She picked up another éclair, pushed the pastry tube into the end, and filled the long puff pastry with cream.

Lenora shook her head, making her pink hairnet sway slightly. "Don't worry none about it. Right now, it's a good thing we *don't* have people stampeding in and wanting your event-planning hoopla. We're plenty busy enough."

Jillian smiled at the tall woman's broad, kind face. "You're right, of course. But there are a lot of questions left about what went on."

"And you can't leave a question unanswered," Lenora said, chuckling. "You've been that way since you were a little bitty thing. It drove your teachers crazy, as I remember."

"Maybe," Jillian admitted. She waved the filled éclair as she spoke. "I'm missing something. I know I am, but I'll sort it out."

Lenora laughed again. "I'm sure you will, but you might want to stop waving that éclair before you throw it clean on the floor." The tall woman turned and headed for the door to the front.

Jillian looked at her hand, where the éclair looked a little worse for wear from the waving. Her cheeks warmed as she quickly dunked the top of the éclair in chocolate to hide the evidence and put it on the tray. After that, she made a real effort to focus on the tasks at hand, but questions kept inching their way into her head. By the time she finished filling the trays, she knew she had to do something to find the answers.

"I'm going to take a walk," Jillian called out to her grandmother, who was mixing sugar-cookie dough. "I'll be back for my next assignment in a little while."

Bertie didn't even look up from her mixing bowl. "Fine. I'll have cookies for you to decorate when you get back."

"I'm sure you will," Jillian murmured before slipping out the back door.

The small parking lot where the bakery employees parked was quiet, though Jillian spotted a discarded plastic bag skidding across the pavement as the wind pushed it. She walked over and snagged it, tossing it into a trash can as she walked up the narrow alley that ran along one side of the bakery. She paused next to the bakery's side door and leaned against the wall, pulling her cell phone out of her pocket.

Mrs. Blackwater was still in Jillian's contact list, and she answered on the second ring with an imperious "Yes?"

"This is Jillian Green. I wanted to ask you about the vendors you requested for the wedding. I was wondering about the florist."

"The florist?" Mrs. Blackwater echoed. "They did an adequate job, as far as I could tell. The arrangements at the rehearsal dinner were quite inspired."

Jillian refrained from mentioning that her great-aunt had made the displays, turning the question instead to the florists themselves. "Actually, I was wondering about the florists themselves. Did you know they were related to Jacob Zimmer?"

There was a long pause. "I did not know that. The florist was Alice's idea. She didn't mention why."

"Alice knew they were Jacob's sisters?"

"Sisters? I don't know. I cannot imagine that she wouldn't,"

Mrs. Blackwater said. "My daughter has odd ideas sometimes. She probably thought she was doing a good deed." Jillian heard a rustling on the phone. "Oh, here is my daughter now. I'll let you ask her yourself."

Jillian heard Mrs. Blackwater briefly explain who was on the phone, making Jillian sound inappropriately eccentric for calling.

The snotty tone was interrupted suddenly when Alice Blackwater spoke into the phone, sounding almost breathless. "Hi, Jillian! Do you have something to report?"

"Nothing new," Jillian said. "Assuming you got my e-mail about the swamp."

"I did." Alice's tone turned angry. "I cannot believe no one is launching a proper search of the swamp for Gordon."

"Unfortunately, the hat is the only sign he was ever there," Jillian said. "No one saw him, and the park requires visitors to sign in and get tickets."

Alice sniffed. "They aren't very careful about it."

"I wanted to ask you about something else," Jillian said, then explained about running into Rose and learning she was Jacob's sister. She skipped over any mention of the paranormal society, feeling that was better left unsaid.

"I didn't know Rose was in town. She worked for a video production company in Atlanta. I thought she was really happy there," Alice said in surprise. "I included Lilly's business to honor Jacob. I didn't know either of the sisters all that well. Jacob introduced us, of course, but Rose lived in Atlanta. And, honestly, Lilly always seemed a little odd to me."

"Odd how?" Jillian asked.

"Well, Jacob told me she was afraid of cats. Can you imagine being afraid of my darling Chess?"

Actually, having seen Lilly react to Possum, she could imagine Lilly would react similarly to Chess. Then she thought of something else she'd wondered about. "I've talked to some people who knew Jacob. They said his antique shop kept odd hours."

"Jacob hardly ever opened the shop," Alice agreed. "I don't think he was there more than once a week. I loved that he had so much flexibility, considering we were planning a wedding, but Daddy thought it showed a poor work ethic."

"How did he make any money opening only once a week?" Jillian asked.

"You sound like Daddy," Alice said, her tone miffed. "Jacob told me most of his business was for private clients. He said he connected people with the things they wanted. I thought that sounded wonderful, like a fairy godmother. Or I guess it would have been a godfather." She sighed. "I miss Jacob so much. I miss Gordon. I don't know why this keeps happening, but I'm glad you're looking into it for me. I know you'll find answers."

Jillian wished she felt as confident. "What happened to his antique shop?"

"It's closed," Alice said. "He owned the building, and he hasn't been missing long enough to be declared dead, so it's just closed. I guess his sisters will own it eventually. Right now, it's a creepy old building at the edge of town."

"I don't suppose you have a key to get in?"

"Me? No. I don't know who would. Maybe Lilly? I was only in the shop a couple of times, and I didn't see anything that struck me as very nice."

"Could you give me the address for the shop?" Jillian asked.

"Sure." Alice rattled off the address, then dropped her voice. "Mother is waving at me, so I best give her back the phone. Thank you for continuing to search for Gordon. I don't know what I'd do without you."

"I don't know that I'm going to find anything," Jillian said, not wanting to give Alice false hope.

"You will. I can feel it." Before Jillian could say thing else, the young woman bid her a hasty good-bye and ended the call.

With a sigh, Jillian started to push the phone into her pocket but then stopped. She called up Savannah's name on her contact list and was pleased when her friend answered right away. "Are you up to more sleuthing?"

"You want to head back to the swamp?" Savannah asked.

"No, this time it's closer to home," Jillian said. She caught Savannah up on the Lowland Paranormal Investigators' meeting and what she'd learned. Savannah gasped audibly at the revelation that the florists were the sisters of the missing first fiancé.

"Do you think they might have been behind the ghost of Jacob?" Savannah asked. "If Rose and Lilly weren't fond of Alice, maybe they hatched the idea of wrecking her wedding as a way to get back at her."

"I suppose that's possible," Jillian agreed. "Though they don't strike me as the vindictive type."

"People can surprise you," Savannah said. "So, are we investigating the sisters?"

"Not them. I want to check out Jacob's antique shop. Apparently, it's been closed for the past year since his disappearance. That makes me wonder what information might be inside."

"I don't suppose you have a key," Savannah said.

"Actually, no," Jillian said. "So we'll probably be limited to peering through windows, but I still plan to do it. What do you say? Want to skulk around with me after the bakery closes?"

"I wouldn't miss it for the world."

After ending the call, Jillian shoved the phone back into her pocket and started her walk. Maybe a little exercise would shake loose the cobwebs in her head. She felt strongly that the disappearances of Alice's fiancés were linked somehow, but she couldn't work out how.

"Jillian! Wait up!" Jillian turned to see Laura Lee, neatly dressed in her buff-and-brown deputy uniform with her long hair pulled up into a ponytail. Her friend waved and trotted to catch up to Jillian on the sidewalk. "I haven't seen you since the wedding. How's your head?"

"A little sore," Jillian said. "But no more headaches. I'm sorry I missed the Sweetie Pies meeting."

Laura Lee grinned at her. "Liar. I heard about what you and Savannah were up to, and I know you'd much rather poke around a crime scene than discuss baking techniques with us."

"I had no idea I was going to find a crime scene," Jillian said. "I really did miss the meeting for a headache. I only went to the apartment in response to blackmail."

"Blackmail?" Laura Lee's eyes widened, and she tapped the badge pinned to her uniform. "You do know I'm in law enforcement, right?"

Jillian laughed. "Not that kind of blackmail. More like emotional blackmail, from Alice Blackwater. The poor thing was a wreck, and I can't blame her. Imagine having two different fiancés up and vanish before the weddings."

"I can't imagine having two fiancés, must less the rest of it."

"You haven't heard anything about Gordon's disappearance, have you?" Jillian asked.

"Besides the rantings of Deputy Jones at finding you at a crime scene?"

"Yeah, besides that. Alice is still so worried about Gordon, and finding blood on his steering wheel wasn't exactly comforting."

Laura Lee gave her a long look, then dropped her voice. "You know Gooder would kill me for talking about it."

"I don't want to get you in trouble," Jillian said; she really wanted to shake her friend until she spilled everything she knew, but she didn't want to learn it at the expense of Laura Lee's job.

The younger woman shrugged. "No big deal really. The blood on the steering wheel was Gordon's, but there was very little of it. It could have been from something as small as a nosebleed. But, there was an interesting e-mail on Gordon's laptop."

"An e-mail?"

"From one of those free e-mail accounts. We haven't had much luck finding out who sent it. It was hard to track."

Jillian again felt like shaking her friend. "What did it say?"

"It said, 'You'll pay for what you did.'"

A cold chill ran through Jillian at the simple words. Is that why Gordon disappeared? Had someone made him pay for what he did? And was that payment related to Jacob's disappearance somehow?

"Was that all?"

The young deputy crossed her arms over her chest and nodded. "Yeah. It wasn't exactly informative, but I have to admit, it sounded creepy to me. Gooder pointed out that it only sounds ominous when you couple it with Gordon's disappearance. It could be related to work or some dispute with a neighbor."

"I don't know," Jillian said. "I believe I would find that pretty scary if it turned up on my computer." She remembered that she had gotten an ominous e-mail on her computer, and it had come from one of the free online e-mail providers too. Could they be related? She rubbed her arms as goose bumps raised on her skin.

Laura Lee didn't seem to notice her reaction. "On a related note, the hat in the swamp didn't turn up anything new either. No one saw Gordon in the swamp, and his car shows no signs of having been in the swamp recently. This time of year, cars that visit the swamp pick up very specific pollen." She shrugged.

"So someone dressed like a dead man and showed up at Gordon's rehearsal dinner," Jillian said. "And later, someone sends him a vaguely threatening e-mail about something he did, maybe in secret. And then, someone tossed his apartment and tore up a photo of Gordon and Jacob. If those pieces fit together, it suggests Gordon might be involved in Jacob Zimmer's disappearance."

"Maybe. Or maybe someone was pranking Gordon because they have a sick sense of humor. Maybe he took off because he got cold feet. Maybe one of his neighbors caught him putting recycling in the trash bin and intends to turn him in to the super. Honestly, we don't know."

Jillian frowned. "You sound like Gooder."

"That's not the world's worst thing," Laura Lee said. "He doesn't appreciate you much, but he's not a bad cop."

"I know. I feel these two disappearances are connected, that's all."

Laura Lee shrugged. "Well, there is something to be said for going with what your gut is telling you. Just don't let Deputy Jones know that you're poking around the edges of one of his cases. I worry about his blood pressure where you're concerned." She reached out and patted Jillian's arm firmly. "I got to run, but if you really think the disappearance of these two guys is connected, you be careful. We don't need you disappearing too."

"I'll do my best," Jillian said. Then before Laura Lee could dash off, she added, "Oh, I do have one other thing."

"What's that?"

"Could you find out the e-mail address for me?" Jillian asked.

"Probably, but it doesn't exist anymore. The sender closed it down."

"That's all right," Jillian said. "Do you know the address or can you find it?"

"Sure, I'll text you when I dig it up. Now, I really have to run."

"Thanks." Jillian watched her friend stride away. Though the early spring weather wasn't overly hot yet, Jillian was still pretty sure that she'd be a sweaty mess if she rushed around the streets that way. *Life isn't fair.*

When she got back to the bakery, she found several pans of egg-shaped cookies waiting for her to decorate them in pastel colors. The project turned out to be surprisingly therapeutic. She was able to put ghosts and swamps and threatening e-mails out of her head for a while as she carefully piped tiny flowers and ribbons on the sugar cookies. When she finished, she decorated a couple of birthday cakes.

Bertie looked over the cakes and gave Jillian a mild compliment. Jillian hoped the good day was going to extend through her plans with Savannah.

Late in the day, Jillian was cleaning up the decorating table, wiping away flecks of color with a warm, wet rag, when Maggie peeked around the doorway from the front. "Savannah is here," she called out. "She said to take as long as you need, because she's going to sit down with a muffin and coffee."

Jillian looked up at the clock in surprise. She hadn't realized the day had passed so quickly. She finished her cleaning, then walked back to the storeroom, where Bertie was making a list of supplies for her monthly order. Jillian stood in the storage room door for a moment, watching her grandmother work.

Bertie was a little woman, standing barely shoulder height to Jillian, but she certainly made a powerful impression. That was something she had in common with her twin sister. Jillian realized she owed much of her personality to the sisters. She was stubborn like her grandmother, but she had Cornelia's adventurous streak.

Looking up from a stack of flour sacks, Bertie caught sight of her and raised her eyebrows. "You need something?"

"I thought I'd see if you needed my help to close," Jillian said. "Savannah is here. We're planning to go out."

Bertie grunted. "I think Lenora and Maggie can close the shop for the day. I'm here until I get this inventory done. It shouldn't be much longer." Her expression softened. "I'm glad you and Savannah have plans, though I wouldn't mind hearing that you and Hunter had plans."

Jillian felt a pang of guilt. "I should call Hunter and see how he's doing."

"Good thinking. You could do that before you leave today."

Jillian couldn't humor Bertie's matchmaking impulses *that* much. "Since Savannah is waiting for me, I think I'll wait until I get home."

"Whatever you think is best," Bertie said, turning back to her list and waving vaguely in Jillian's direction.

I guess I've been dismissed.

Jillian walked through the bakery, untying her apron and pulling it over her head as she walked. She hung it on the hook inside the doorway to the front area where most of the tables were filled with customers chatting and nibbling pastries.

With a spike of pure panic, Jillian froze as she spotted Maudie Honeycutt and Wanda Jean Maplewood at one of the tables, their faces turned toward Savannah, who stood nearby chatting. Jillian was fond of Maudie and Wanda Jean, but the two best friends would be absolutely impossible to shake off if they knew Jillian and Savannah were going to look for clues at Jacob's antique shop.

Pasting a smile on her face, she walked over to the table. "Are we having a mini meeting of the Sweetie Pies today?" she asked brightly.

Maudie shifted her attention to Jillian. Her snow-white pixie cut and bright eyes made her look like Peter Pan's grandmother. "I ran into Bertie at the grocery store yesterday, and she told me you finally conquered brownies. So Wanda Jean and I thought we'd stop by and try them out." She held up half a brownie. "It's yummy."

"It is good," Wanda Jean agreed, though her sharp-eyed gaze made Jillian nervous. She knew the look of Wanda Jean on a mission. "But I'm more interested in the excitement at the wedding. I hope you're feeling better."

Jillian nodded, carefully holding on to the smile. "Other than being forced into creative hairstyling, I'm fine. Back to normal."

"Well, that's good," Wanda Jean said. "Didn't I hear you had some excitement on a day trip with Savannah? Something about an alligator? Whatever were you two doing in the swamp?"

Savannah fielded the question neatly. "Jillian hadn't been out there. The Okefenokee National Wildlife Refuge has fascinating old swamper cabins. It's a part of history we don't think about very much."

"I didn't know you were interested in history," Maudie said, her eyes still on Jillian. "Bertie says you don't pay enough attention to family history."

"It's possible my grandmother just enjoys complaining," Jillian said. "Though Savannah is much more of a history buff than I am. I did enjoy a day away from the bakery to recover from my knock on the head."

Disappointment dulled the shine in Wanda Jean's eyes. "I'm sure it was a lovely day, in spite of the alligator."

Maudie turned toward her friend. "Maybe you and I should go sometime. I love historical displays, and the alligators sound exciting."

"Maybe," Wanda Jean said, before shoving more brownie into her mouth.

With the disaster averted, Jillian relaxed slightly and turned toward Savannah. "Did you want to get a snack before we go?"

Savannah shook her head. "No, I'm fine." She smiled down at Wanda Jean and Maudie. "See y'all on Sunday."

Wanda Jean looked pointedly at Jillian. "I hope to see you at the next Sweetie Pie meeting too."

"I'll be there," Jillian promised, then snagged Savannah's arm, and they managed to make it out of the bakery before anyone else engaged them in conversation.

Once they hit the sidewalk, Jillian spoke quietly. "I was terrified we were going to have two extra sleuths on this expedition."

"I don't doubt that we would have if Wanda Jean had caught wind of what we were doing," Savannah said. "I could practically feel her bloodhound instincts kicking in. By the way, I parked in the back alley. Do you want to take my car or yours?"

"Let's take mine," Jillian said. "I'll drive you back after we check out the antique shop, unless you want to get some dinner with me?"

"I'm always up for dinner," Savannah said cheerfully. "It beats eating alone."

Jillian glanced sideways at her friend. "I'm surprised you eat alone much. I thought you and James would end up together."

"I thought so too," Savannah said. "I guess we were friends for so long, it just seems to be the right setting for our relationship." She shrugged. "I'm in no hurry. I enjoy my life."

Jillian had to admit that she liked her own single life as well, something she thought about often when Bertie was putting the full-court press on her about Hunter Greyson. Despite what her grandmother thought, Jillian wasn't opposed to the idea of romance. But she wasn't in a hurry for it either.

When the two women reached the parking lot, Jillian's phone vibrated in her pocket, alerting her to a text message. She pulled out the phone and checked. Laura Lee had passed along the e-mail address from the mysterious message on Gordon's computer. Jillian had expected it to match the e-mail address from the threat she'd received, but it didn't. It wasn't even the same free e-mail provider.

"Something wrong?" Savannah asked.

Jillian explained about the conversation she'd had with Laura

Lee. "I really thought the e-mail on the threatening message to Gordon would match the one I got."

"It didn't?"

Jillian shook her head as she slipped her phone back in her pocket. "No, it wasn't even the same e-mail provider. I guess I still don't have any clues to who 'Spirit of Vengeance' could be."

Savannah's brows raised in surprise. "You got an e-mail from Spirit of Vengeance? That's the name of a video game."

"How would you know that?"

Savannah laughed. "One of my clients has a teenage son who loves the game. He plays it constantly; it's all he talks about." She stopped talking, and her eyes went wide. "What did the e-mail say?"

"Luckily, I have obsessed about it enough to memorize it. Though I'm sure it didn't come from some teenager." Jillian closed her eyes, taking a moment to call up the exact wording. "'Don't think there won't be repercussions for what you decided to do. If you want to survive, you'll stick to your own business!'"

Savannah burst out laughing.

"You find my death threat funny?" Jillian asked.

Savannah shook her head. "No, I find it funny because I'm pretty sure it's not a death threat. The teenager who loves that game is Trenton Meyer. His father owns Dreams Come True."

"Richard Meyer's son is threatening me?" Jillian asked.

"I doubt it. I expect Richard didn't realize his computer was logged into the wrong account when he sent you an e-mail telling you to stick to the bakery business instead of the wedding-planning business. It's your business he thinks won't survive, not you."

"You think so?" Jillian asked. "I don't know. That language was pretty harsh."

"I only know of one way to be sure. Let's make a quick stop on the way to the antique store. We can ask Richard directly, because I'm sure *that* is where the e-mail came from."

"Fine," Jillian said, though she wasn't sure it was fine at all as she got into the car.

Savannah was correct that Richard Meyer's house was on the way to their destination. The location effectively split the distance between the bakery and the antique shop in half. The wedding planner lived in a neat, two-story bungalow with a beautifully landscaped yard.

"This place certainly is pretty," Jillian said as she peered up at the house from the driveway.

"Come on," Savannah said as she swung open her door. "He doesn't bite. I promise."

"I don't know," Jillian said. "He got kind of snappy at Crazy Fish."

Savannah headed up the driveway to the flagstone sidewalk, forcing Jillian out of the car to follow. As Savannah rang the doorbell, Jillian shifted nervously from foot to foot. The door swung open, and the slightly built man who'd confronted Jillian in the restaurant appeared. She had to admit, he looked far less formidable with the warm smile he turned on Savannah.

"Richard," Savannah said, taking his hand. "My friend has a question to ask you."

The wedding planner's gaze moved to Jillian, and his warm smile vanished. "Yes?"

Jillian cleared her throat and quickly launched into a description of the e-mail and the address. "Did you send that e-mail? Are you threatening my life?"

Richard's eyes widened in shock, then his cheeks flushed. "No, of course not. I admit, now that I hear the e-mail spoken aloud, it does sound a little ominous, but that isn't what I meant at all."

"So you weren't threatening to harm me?" Jillian asked. "Just my business."

He held up his hands. "No, I wasn't going to harm anything. I only meant that loyalty matters a lot in business." He shifted slightly, and his voice took on a firmer tone. "And you were very disloyal in starting a wedding-planning business."

"I didn't start a wedding-planning business," Jillian said. "I don't want a wedding-planning business. I want Belle Haven to be open to events; that's all. Then the Blackwaters showed up, and they didn't want to pay a wedding planner, and the whole thing turned into a catastrophe. But Bertie did recommend your business at the very first meeting with Mrs. Blackwater."

The wedding planner's expression softened. "She did?"

"She did," Jillian said. "I know we should have been firmer about it. I promise, I will never take on another wedding at Belle Haven where there isn't a planner. I do *not* want to do your job."

A slight smile appeared on the man's face. "Well, thank you. I'm sorry I was rude. I should have given you a chance to explain the misunderstanding before I flew off the handle."

Savannah smiled at Richard. "You also need to be sure you check what e-mail account you're sending from. It didn't help the confusion when Jillian got an e-mail from 'Spirit of Vengeance.'"

Richard visibly reddened. "No wonder you were upset. I really am sorry." Now it was his turn to shift nervously from foot to foot. "Please, come in and have some coffee."

"That sounds great," Jillian said, "but we have to be somewhere else. I'm glad we got this settled, though."

After another quick apology and a warm handshake, Jillian and Savannah turned away and headed back to the car. As they drove the rest of the way to the antique shop, Jillian marveled at how much lighter she felt at solving one small part of the mystery.

They pulled up in front of a small, boxy building nestled in a wooded lowlands area where many of the trees sported signs insisting no fishing, hunting, or trespassing was allowed. A similar No Trespassing sign taped to the front door had yellowed and hung cockeyed. A few rough boards hung over the windows, but plenty of grubby glass could be seen in gaps between the boards. The parking lot curled around one side of the building and disappeared into the back, featuring uneven pavement with weeds growing up in hopeful clusters through gaping cracks.

"I'm surprised none of the windows are broken," Jillian said as they climbed out of the car.

"We're not exactly in a busy area of town," Savannah answered, shaking her head. "Putting a business way out here makes no sense. He couldn't have gotten any foot traffic at all."

"Alice said he did business mostly with private buyers," Jillian said.

They crossed the small parking lot quickly. She tried to peek into the building between the boards, but the darkness inside offered nothing but shadows.

Straight on, the building looked small, but the shoe-box shape meant it extended back farther than appearances suggested. The actual storefront had a rough wooden step up to the front door. A large display window to the left of the door sported ornate wooden trim that had grown faded and chipped by weather. Part of the facade under the window had fallen away, and Jillian squatted to look into the crawl space under the shop. A maze of pipes and spiderwebs pretty much guaranteed she wouldn't be crawling under there. She saw someone had stashed several five-gallon buckets in the crawl space, but something had knocked them over. With a shudder, she wondered if wild creatures had turned them into housing.

Savannah stepped around her and tried the front door, but it was locked securely. She leaned close, nearly pressing her nose against the smeared glass. "It sure is dark in there."

"I doubt the power is on," Jillian said. "Still, I wish we could get in."

Savannah shrugged. "The front door might not be the only way in."

"I do enjoy how your mind works." They walked around to the far side, away from the parking lot. Climbing ivy had been working on the brick at the side of the building, and Jillian could see crumbling mortar between the thick vines. Near the back of the building, narrow windows were half-covered with the heavy foliage.

"Those haven't been boarded up," Savannah said, pointing.

Jillian reached up and pulled at one of the thick ropes of ivy. The vine barely moved. "Because nature did it for them. Unless we want to come back with a hacksaw, I don't think we'll be getting in through either of these windows."

"A hacksaw might be a thought if we don't find another way in," Savannah said.

"You're taking to this breaking-and-entering thing with a lot more excitement than you did at Gordon's apartment."

"That was a possible crime scene," Savannah said. "This is simply a creepy old building, and I *love* creepy old buildings. Really, if we don't break anything, the worse we'll get is fined for trespassing."

"I suppose."

They waded through the high grass to the back of the building. Jillian kept a sharp eye out for snakes as she walked. She jumped with a shriek when one of the ivy vines hanging from the wall tickled the back of her neck after she stepped too close to the building.

To their surprise, the back of the building was far less overgrown than the front. In fact, someone had recently trimmed the weeds between the back door and the edge of the parking lot. Savannah poked at a pile of dead, trimmed vegetation with the toe of her sneaker.

"Maybe Jacob's sisters were here," Jillian said. "They might have keys to the shop."

"Do you think they'd let you in?" Savannah asked.

Jillian shook her head. "I doubt it. Rose was upset with me for not letting the paranormal people look for Jacob at Belle Haven."

"Did you explain to her that it wasn't a real ghost?"

"I did," Jillian said. "You know, she seemed a sensible person, but I guess grief can make even sensible people a little crazy." She walked the rest of the way to the concrete pad that formed the backdoor landing. The door itself was metal with chipped gray paint and rust spots. A shiny new padlock hung from the door's rusty hasp. She tapped the lock, sending it swinging slightly. "Another sign that someone has been here recently."

"What if it isn't Jacob's sisters?" Savannah asked. "What if it's Jacob?"

"Dead Jacob? I really don't think he's shopping at the hardware store."

"Not if he's dead, of course, but what if he isn't? What if he's alive and back in Moss Hollow secretly? That would explain why Alice was so sure the ghost at the rehearsal dinner was Jacob. Maybe it was."

"So Jacob is playing ghost? That seems rather cruel." Jillian pulled hard on the lock. The hasp moved slightly, making it clear that time and weather had made it less secure in the door, but it didn't move enough for her to imagine she could pull it free. "I wish we could get inside. I still think there may be answers in there."

"We still have one more side of the building to examine. I don't remember seeing all the ivy on that side when we pulled in."

"But I do remember seeing boards over the windows," Jillian said as they tromped through the grass to the edge of the parking lot and walked around the corner to see the last side of the building. As she had remembered, boards were nailed haphazardly over the windows. On one, only a single board ran crosswise over the window, and Jillian could see this was the only window that showed signs of vandalism. The glass behind the board had broken edges.

"Well, that explains why the windows on the other side weren't boarded up," Savannah said. "Someone ran out of boards."

"Which could be our answer," Jillian said. "I have a pry bar in the trunk. Surely we could pull off one little board, nailed in by someone with a questionable work ethic."

"Maybe, but I can't reach that." Savannah walked over to prove it. She stood against the side of the building and reached as high as possible, her fingers overlapping the bottom of the window by only a couple of inches.

Jillian swallowed, not liking the idea she suddenly had. "We could possibly stand on the five-gallon buckets I saw in the crawl space under the shop."

"A wobbly bucket wouldn't be a very good perch," Savannah said.

"It's the only option available. I'll stand on them, and you can spot me so I don't fall. It's not actually the standing that is going to be a problem. It's crawling under the building to get them."

"I can manage that," Savannah said.

Jillian hoped she would still feel that way after seeing how disgusting the crawl space was.

Though Savannah peered into the dark hole without enthusiasm, she dropped to her knees and crawled in. Snagging the handle of a bucket and hauling it behind her, she crawled back out. She repeated the action again. "Will two be enough?"

Jillian looked over the buckets. In the fading light, it was hard to tell. One had a definite crack. "I hate to say it, but it might be best to have all three."

"No problem," Savannah said gamely and crawled back into the hole. "By the way, you're paying for these pants."

"Fair enough."

Jillian saw Savannah snag the handle and begin backing toward the opening. Something shot out of the bucket as soon as it moved, and Savannah screamed. The creature turned sharply, and Jillian was terrified that it was going to attack. She still couldn't tell what it was. It was too big for a rat, but she knew it could be a raccoon or a skunk.

Oh, no, not a skunk, please.

Savannah scrambled out of the hole, still clutching the handle of the bucket. The creature in the crawl space yowled after her, and Jillian nearly fainted from relief. She knew that sound. It was a cat.

She pressed a hand to her chest. "I was afraid that was a skunk."

"The idea passed my mind too," Savannah said. She bent down to peer in the hole. "Do you think the poor thing is all right? I hate to leave it. Kitty, kitty, kitty."

"If it's feral, it probably won't come to you," Jillian said. "And if it's rabid, we'd rather it didn't. Let's see about that window."

Savannah stood again and dusted off the knees of her pants, though dark stains remained behind. "Fine, but I'm coming back with some cat food."

They carried the buckets back to the window, and Jillian retrieved the crowbar from her trunk. Bertie had bought her the crowbar right after her first encounter with a killer in Moss Hollow when Jillian refused to get a gun. She insisted that Jillian needed some kind of weapon in her car if she was going to rush into trouble. At least it was finally going to prove useful.

When she carried it back to the window, Savannah had set up the buckets underneath and had laid a board across them.

"Where did you get the board?" Jillian asked.

"It may or may not have been about ready to fall off one of the front windows," Savannah answered. "But it will help distribute your weight so you don't punch a foot through the bottom of a bucket."

"Sounds good." Jillian climbed on the board. The board had broken lengthwise somewhere along the way, leaving her a fairly narrow place for her feet. She wished she wasn't quite so wobbly, but Savannah put her hands on Jillian's lower back, and she immediately felt much more secure. "Let's give this a try."

She wedged the end of the crowbar under the board, wiggling it back and forth to get it as far under as possible. Then she threw her weight against the end, levering the board several groaning inches away from the wood, but the action also overbalanced Jillian. She would have ended up falling hard if Savannah hadn't taken most of her weight, allowing both of them to stay on their feet. "That was fun," Savannah said.

"I'm glad I didn't land on you," Jillian answered. "Having had a grown adult land on me recently, I don't recommend it."

Savannah gave her a saucy grin. "I would think you'd enjoy having Hunter bump into you now and then."

"Not that hard." Jillian positioned the board back onto the buckets and climbed back up. Again Savannah steadied her. Jillian grabbed the bottom of the board on the window and pulled. The nails gave way, and the board pulled free at the bottom. Jillian hung on, which kept her from falling off the buckets again. She pushed the board sideways, and the upper end groaned as it partly pulled free from the top of the window, leaving it clear enough for someone to crawl through. "That should do it."

"We can get in?" Savannah asked.

"Let me clear the broken glass." She used the crowbar to knock the ragged shards out of the window. In the rapidly dying light, it was hard to be sure the window frame was completely safe, but she didn't see any more glass. She turned to look back at Savannah. "Can you give me a boost?"

Savannah laced her fingers to form a stirrup, and Jillian stepped up and grabbed the window frame, pulling herself through. She felt something bite into her left hand and realized she must have missed a piece of glass, but she ignored the pain and wriggled through the window and onto a wooden table half full of dusty junk.

When the table took her weight without complaint, Jillian turned and reached out with her right hand. "Let me pull you up."

"On three." Savannah hopped up on the board across the buckets. "One, two, three!" She jumped, letting Jillian haul her through the window. The weight of both women was too much for the old table, and one of the legs buckled, spilling them onto the floor in a pile. They untangled from each other and stood. "You all right?" Savannah asked.

"I cut my hand on some glass, but it's nothing." Jillian looked at the busted table. "Well, so much for not breaking anything."

"Let me take a look at that hand." Savannah pulled out a flashlight that couldn't have been more than a couple of inches long. "Always be prepared," Savannah said. "There doesn't seem to be any glass in the wound, and it's mostly stopped bleeding. You'll need to wash it out as soon as you can."

"I doubt the water is still running here," Jillian said, then smiled. "But we're inside. Time to look for clues."

"What exactly are we looking for?" Savannah asked.

"I'm not sure," Jillian admitted. "But if Jacob's disappearance began everything, we're looking for anything that will help us understand it." She looked around the small room and saw cheap shelf units lined the walls. Various objects filled most of the shelves. Besides the table that lay in ruins on the floor, there was a small, cheap-looking desk and a chair. "Do you think this was the shop's office?"

Savannah shone her light around the room, finally lingering on the desk. "Maybe. So we search the desk?"

"We search the desk." They crossed the small room, and Savannah shone her tiny light on the desk so Jillian could look at the various papers. They looked like ordinary records of purchases and sales. Jacob had picked up items at yard sales and estate sales, according to the notes made on some of the papers. By the time she'd gone through all the papers on top of the desk, she had learned absolutely nothing of value.

"Maybe he kept the secret stuff in the drawers," Savannah suggested, pulling open one of the drawers and shining a light in.

A low moaning sound followed by loud thumps came from the other side of the door to the small room. The women exchanged alarmed looks.

They weren't alone.

"What do you think that is?" Savannah whispered. The moaning sounded frantic, and the thumping grew even louder. "Maybe someone is trying to scare us?"

"We're trespassing. Why try to scare us when they could come in and demand we leave?" Jillian had to speak in a loud whisper to be heard over the thumps. "I think we should go see what's making the noise."

"Really?"

"Really."

The two women walked to the door, practically huddled together. Jillian wrapped her hand around the doorknob. She knew this was one of those moments when she would be yelling at the heroine of any scary movie, urging her not to open the door. But if you don't open it, you never find out what's on the other side. Jillian *had* to find out.

Jillian turned the knob slowly. Behind them, they heard a loud thump, followed by more crashing. Jillian and Savannah shrieked in unison and turned to face the new danger.

18

The tiny light of Savannah's flashlight barely reached across the small room, doing little more than lifting the shadows a bit. It was enough. In the debris from the falling table, the scrawny cat from under the crawl space glared at them. As the dim glow flashed across the cat's face, its eyes glowed red.

Jillian bent over and put her hands on her knees, trying to catch her breath from the leftover fear. "I'm beginning to understand how someone could develop a cat phobia."

"The poor thing didn't want to be left behind," Savannah said. "Did you, baby?" She took a step toward the cat when the sound of more thumping on the other side of the door jerked their attention back to the mystery of what lay beyond.

"Fine," Jillian said. "I'm done being scared." She jerked open the door and stepped into a dark, narrow hallway. Savannah crowded behind her and shone her light in all directions. On the right end of the hall, they could see the back door leading outside. On the left end, a beaded curtain made a kind of door to the main area of the antique shop. Directly across the hall, they faced a door that was nearly identical to the one they'd just opened.

"Which way?" Savannah whispered.

The sound, which had stopped when they opened the door, started back up again. The thumps and moans were coming from the other side of the door they faced. "Forward!"

Jillian opened the door. Savannah shone the light into the space. They saw a large bathroom area, with more shelving along the farthest wall.

They also saw a man, tied up and gagged in a straight-backed chair.

It was Gordon Liddell. He was filthy with a huge bruised bump on his forehead.

"Gordon!" Jillian said.

While Savannah stood in the doorway to shine her flashlight into the room, Jillian rushed across the room and pulled the gag out of his mouth. "How did you get in here?"

Gordon tried to speak, but his voice came out as a rough croak. "Water?"

Jillian turned to the sink, but as she'd expected, no water came out.

"I think I saw some bottled water in the office," Savannah said. "I'll go get a bottle."

Jillian nodded and began picking at the knots that held Gordon to the chair. "Did you recognize the people who did this to you?" she asked.

He shook his head and croaked out, "Never saw them."

"You never saw who grabbed you?"

He shook his head again and winced. Even with the ivy, the windows in the room let in enough light to see he was licking his lips and swallowing. Finally he said, "Someone hid in my car. Knocked me senseless and pulled a hood over my head."

"Well, at least we found you," Jillian said. "I know Alice will be glad to hear that."

He looked at Jillian, his expression eager. "Alice is all right?"

"She's fine. Worried about you."

He closed his eyes for a moment before whispering, "I was so worried."

"I don't doubt it. Let's focus on getting you out of here before your captor comes back." She looked up at his face. "Could Jacob have been the person who grabbed you?"

For the first time, his expression turned guarded. "Jacob's dead."

"But his body was never found," Jillian reminded him. She

heard footsteps in the hall and turned toward the doorway, expecting to see Savannah with the bottle of water.

Instead, she found herself looking straight into the angry face of Lilly Quest.

Jillian's eyes dropped to the gun Lilly held pointed directly at her. "Get away from him," Lilly demanded.

"Lilly?" Jillian said. "What are you doing? You kidnapped Gordon?"

"He killed my brother." The gun barrel pointed at Gordon. "He killed him and left his body in the swamp. And he's going to tell me where."

"I didn't kill Jacob," Gordon said frantically. "I swear."

"Liar," Lilly growled. "You killed him so you could have Alice. You knew she would never pick you over Jacob."

Gordon swallowed hard. "I did know that. But I didn't kill Jacob. He was my friend."

"Friend! It was you," Lilly said. "No one else had a reason."

"That's not true," Gordon insisted. "Jacob was involved with some bad people."

Lilly took another step closer and roared at him. "You're lying!"

"I'm not! I swear!"

With Lilly nearly trembling with rage, Jillian knew she had to do something fast or Gordon was going to get shot. *And probably me too.* But rushing a woman with a gun didn't seem to be a good plan.

"Lilly?"

Lilly whirled to face the doorway, just as Savannah jumped to the side and tossed something into the room, low to the floor. The something turned out to be the stray cat, who yowled in complaint at the rude treatment and raced toward the windows. The cat's path took it directly toward Lilly.

Lilly screamed, throwing her hands up in panic.

Jillian took the opportunity to tackle the florist, and Lilly dropped the gun, sending it skidding across the floor. Savannah rushed into the room to help Jillian.

"Get me loose!" Gordon screamed.

"Get the gun!" Jillian yelled as she tried to hold down the squirming florist.

Savannah had reached the struggling woman and looked into Jillian's eyes. "Where's the gun?"

"I have it."

Everyone in the room turned toward the door. Rose stood in the doorway, the gun hanging loosely from her hand by her side. At the sight of her, Jillian scrambled off Lilly and knelt on the floor next to Gordon.

Lilly sat up, looking frantically around the room as she scooted toward one of the walls and pressed her back against it. "The cat," she cried. "Rose, you have to shoot it before it gets me."

"It's not going to get you," Rose said gently. "No one is going to get you." She looked at Savannah. "Would you get the cat, please?"

Jillian thought the *please* was a nice touch, even though they were hardly likely to refuse the orders of a woman with a gun.

Savannah walked over to the corner where the cat crouched and watched them warily. She scooped up the cat. Surprisingly, it didn't scratch her.

Lilly took one look at the cat and began to whimper. She scooted along the wall until she came to the corner of the room, as far from the animal as the room allowed. With her eyes still on the cat, she spoke to her sister in a breathless voice. "You have to tie them up. Then we can make Gordon tell us where he hid Jacob's body."

"Gordon didn't hide Jacob's body," Rose said gently.

"Of course he did," Lilly insisted. "He must have. You know that."

Rose shook her head. "We were wrong." She stepped aside, making room for a young man to step in. Even though the room was growing still darker, Jillian recognized the man in the door immediately. She'd never seen him in the flesh, but she had no doubt.

It was Jacob Zimmer.

At the sight of him, Lilly Quest simply fainted.

Sorting out all the details took a while and had to wait until poor Gordon was finally untied and given something to drink. Jacob carried his older sister to a sofa at the front of the antique shop, then lit several old oil lamps to provide light for the discussion. Savannah fetched a bottle of water for Lilly when she regained consciousness.

"Obviously I never killed Jacob," Gordon said as he settled into a chair with his bottle of water, "but I am responsible for his disappearance. I thought I was doing the right thing."

"You were," Jacob said, smiling at his friend as he sat next to his sister, holding her hand as she stared at him in wonder. "Maybe not for totally pure motives, but I'm the one who got myself into a bad spot, not you." He looked at the faces that watched him, then sadly down at his older sister. "What he said is true. I did get involved with some bad people."

Lilly shook her head slowly but whispered, "Why? How?"

"The first time, it seemed innocent enough. I was only putting together a buyer and a seller, and it was just an old figurine. It's not as if I was selling drugs." He dropped his sister's hand and looked down at the floor in front of him. "That's what I told myself. But then I read a news report online about an elderly man who died in a robbery, a robbery that included the little figurine that I had in my shop at that very moment. That's when I realized what I was doing was far from harmless."

"Why didn't you stop?" Lilly asked.

"He couldn't," Rose said.

Jacob nodded. "I tried, but the thieves threatened my family, and they threatened Alice. Then Gordon figured it out. He demanded I leave town or he'd turn me in."

All eyes turned to Gordon, and he looked miserable. "Jacob was acting so strange and secretive, so I followed him to the swamp and saw one of the exchanges. I was so angry when I figured out what he was involved in. I didn't want it to hurt Alice."

"I didn't want that either," Jacob said. "So when Gordon confronted me, I considered running. I even packed my clothes, but then I knew that would only make Alice a bigger target. So I turned myself in to the authorities."

Surprise bloomed on Gordon's and Lilly's faces. "Then why were you gone?" she asked.

"They made me a deal," Jacob said. "Do some undercover work to bust up the blackmarket art and antiquities ring, and they would drop the charges against me. But that meant I had to leave without a word to anyone. I had to let you think I was dead." He looked at Lilly. "I'm so sorry."

"I'm just happy you're alive," Lilly said softly.

"Not me," Rose said. She pointed at her brother. "I'm very annoyed with you. That is not the way twins treat each other." She gave Jillian a guilty look. "Not that Lilly and I are blameless. I do makeup effects for the video company in Atlanta. So I'm the one who disguised Lilly as the ghost of Jacob. We hoped it would freak Gordon out enough to send him running to wherever he buried our brother. We truly believed he had killed Jacob."

"I had no idea what was happening," Gordon said, raising his voice slightly as he looked at Lilly. "Because I didn't bury your brother."

"So were the two of you the ones who sent the threatening e-mail to Gordon?" Jillian asked. "And then you decided to kidnap him?"

"No," Rose said. "I thought Gordon had run for it when he disappeared, marking the end of our last chance for answers."

"So you weren't involved in the kidnapping?" Jillian asked.

"It was only me," Lilly said. She turned to look at Gordon. "I'm so sorry."

"Jacob," Savannah said, speaking for the first time since she'd sat down, "are you done with your undercover work now? I'm sure Alice would want to know you're alive."

Jacob looked at her, his face miserable. "I'm not done yet. I came back because I read about Gordon's disappearance, and I thought maybe the art thieves were involved. I had to find out. Now that I know, I'll have to go finish what I started."

"What do we tell Alice?" Jillian asked.

"Nothing," Jacob said. "I'll talk to her tonight before I leave."

"So the moral of the story is there's no such thing as ghosts," Jillian said as she finished telling Bertie and Cornelia all about the encounter at breakfast the next morning.

"It seems to me that the moral of the story is that secrets can be dangerous," Cornelia said mildly.

"The moral of the story," Bertie interjected, "is to choose a nice, stable guy. Someone you can trust. Someone you can count on. Someone like Hunter Greyson."

"Leave it to you to turn this back into meddling in my love life."

Bertie pointed at Jillian with the butter knife. "You don't have a love life. If you did, I wouldn't meddle."

"Sure you wouldn't," Jillian muttered.

Cornelia rapped on the table with her butter knife for attention. "Back to Jacob and Alice. How did Alice react to the discovery of Jacob's resurrection?"

"I don't know," Jillian admitted. "We didn't go to her house as a group. It was something Jacob needed to do in private."

"Fine. I have another question," Cornelia said. "What happened to the cat? It sounds as if it was quite the hero."

"That is one question I do know the answer to, since it rode in my car. Savannah said she's planning to give it a nice flea bath and find it a good home."

"Why doesn't she give it a good home herself?" Cornelia asked.

"Maybe she will. When I left her, she was cuddling the scrawny thing and calling it Hero."

"She's doomed," Bertie said. "Once you give them a name, there's no going back. That's exactly how it started with Possum."

Jillian slathered butter on her fresh muffin. "Maybe."

At the bakery a few hours later, Maggie came looking for Jillian in the back room where she was wrapping up day-old goods to carry over to the senior center. She was getting a late start, but the morning had been unusually busy.

"Someone out front wants to talk to you," Maggie said.

"Someone?"

Maggie shrugged. "Your client? The mayor's daughter with the crazy-colored hair."

"Ah, that someone." Jillian walked through the back of the bakery, enjoying the smell of bread baking as she passed the big ovens. She found Alice Blackwater standing near the front window, gazing out at the street. "Alice?"

The young woman turned to her, and Jillian saw her red-rimmed eyes. She managed a small smile. "Jillian. I wanted to thank you for finding Gordon and Jacob for me."

"I don't know how much credit I deserve for that."

"You deserve plenty, I'm sure," Alice said. She held out a slip of paper. "I wanted to give you this."

Jillian saw that the young woman was holding out a check. She held up her hands. "You don't owe me anything. Your mother paid all the wedding bills, and I certainly don't need to be paid for trying to help you find answers."

Alice nodded. "I know, but it's not inappropriate to offer a tip for good service. I checked. And it's not a lot, but I wanted to make it clear that I appreciate everything you did. Maybe you can handle my real wedding."

"You're going to marry Gordon?" Jillian asked. "Or will it be Jacob?"

Alice shrugged slightly "I don't know yet. I do love them, both of them. But maybe it won't be either. I'm young. I have plenty of time to figure it out."

Jillian nodded, wishing her grandmother would embrace that attitude. "Well, good luck with whatever you decide." She smiled slightly. "If you do decide to get married, Belle Haven will be happy to host it, but from now on, I only work with a separate wedding planner."

"That's fair." Alice's pale face suddenly bloomed into a mischievous smile. "But I'm not sure that will be enough to keep you out of trouble. I get the feeling things like this are going to follow you no matter what you do."

Jillian looked at Alice in alarm. "I certainly hope not."

"If it does, I'm sure you'll handle it," Alice said. "You seem to be good at handling these adventures." Her gaze turned back to the window, and she smiled again, pointing. "Speaking of which, wasn't that your date for the wedding? Maybe a new adventure is on the way."

Jillian looked out the window and saw Hunter striding purposefully toward the bakery. She took a moment to admire his sure, broad-shouldered posture and beautiful suit. If that was adventure, she had to admit it looked pretty good.

Alice laughed lightly and patted Jillian's arm. "Good luck."

"Thank you," Jillian said quietly. She was pretty sure she'd need it.

Sugar Coated Lies
Book Three Recipe

Jillian's Nemesis Brownies

½ cup butter, cut into pieces
2 ounces semisweet baking
   chocolate
1 cup white sugar
½ cup brown sugar
3 eggs

¼ cup unsweetened cocoa
   powder
½ teaspoon salt
½ cup plus 2 tablespoons flour
½ cup milk chocolate chips

Instructions

Preheat oven to 350 degrees.

1. In a large, microwave-safe bowl, melt the butter and semisweet chocolate in microwave, stirring every 30 seconds until smooth.

2. Whisk the white and brown sugar into the melted chocolate and butter mixture.

3. While the chocolate mixture cools slightly, beat the eggs in a separate bowl. Mix the eggs into the melted chocolate mixture a little at a time until well combined.

4. Mix in the cocoa powder and salt, then fold in the flour until combined. Stir in the chocolate chips.

5. Pour the batter into a parchment-lined, 8-inch-square baking pan.

6. Bake 35 to 40 minutes until a toothpick inserted in the center comes out with moist crumbs.

7. Cool for 15 minutes and remove from pan, transferring to a wire rack to cool completely.

Yield: 9 servings.

Learn more about Annie's fiction books at

AnniesFiction.com

- Access your e-books
- Discover exciting new series
- Read sample chapters
- Watch video book trailers
- Share your feedback

We've designed the Annie's Fiction website especially for you!

Plus, manage your account online!

- Check your account status
- Make payments online
- Update your address

Visit us at AnniesFiction.com